Frost

Michael T. Crawford

For grandma. I wouldn't be half the man I am if it weren't for you. I'll see you again someday.

Prelude

Are you awake?
I don't think so...
Open your eyes.
They're too heavy... too cold.
You've slept for ages.
I have? How?
Try to remember.
I can't... my mind is blank.
Then just wake up.
Who are you?
I am you.
Then who am I?
You should be asking yourself that.
But... aren't you... me?
I am who you used to be.
Used to be?
You have changed... I am not needed.
Need?
You need to wake up.
It's too cold.
Waking from the dead normally is.
I'm dead?
You are. If you wake, you will be born.
You mean reborn?
*No, you are a changed version of my self, but you
have not been given life. You must wake up.*
All right...
Are you scared?
...No.
You should be.

Part I: Brave, New World

Chapter I

The brave, new world has been mankind's dream for a time immeasurable; a place with a united people, each person just as important and special as the next. An age of prosperity in a world of peace. That was the dream, anyway.

The real new world may have been brave, but far from peace or prosperity. A frozen wasteland was all that existed on the God forsaken planet Earth. But, just like the dream world was to be achieved by man, this world was too.

The inhabitants of this world could barely be called people any longer. Mankind was nothing more than bottom-feeding scavengers, rummaging through the snow and ice for food, technology and medicine. Even in this icy hell, however, man stayed true to form, keeping itself as its most hated enemy.

The toll demanded by the new world placed man at odds with itself. Rapidly, the inhabitants had formed gangs, clans, tribes and other organizations. All were bent on controlling as much useless territory as possible, obsessed with finding supplies to allow them to survive for another day longer. What there was to look forward to, however, no one could say.

* * *

Deep beneath the frozen surface of the planet, one such gang, possessing an incredible lust for technology, was searching an old science facility for supplies. It was a small group of men and women, armed with weapons ranging from swords to scythes, flintlock pistols to shotguns. Yet even with the hardened hearts and weapons they possessed, nothing could have prepared them for what laid sleeping within the core of the facility.

"Creepy place, huh, Layla?" one man said. He was tall, lanky and had enough hair to keep cancer treatment patients supplied with wigs for a decade. On his left hip was flintlock pistol and strapped to his back was a large, cruelly curved scythe. Fitted in thick, black leather armor, he was the modern image of the grim reaper.

"Just like a 20th century sci-fi movie, Kyle," the woman, Layla, replied. She was tall, blonde and slender, a perfect specimen for a modeling agency in more peaceful times. Her eyes, however, had the hardened look of one who had killed with a smile on her face time and time again. Her body was wrapped in thick wool strips, adorned with colorful beads and menacing, spiked belts that held the outfit together. On each hip was a short katana, and on her back was a 12-gauge shotgun.

"Think we'll find anything good down here?"

"Nathan's confident we will."

"Yeah, he was also confident about the last two wild-goose chases. Do you think we'll find anything good?"

"Of course we'll find something good!" a voice cut in.

Layla and Kyle turned around to see a broad shouldered, bald, scruffy, dark-skinned man in a thick fur coat approaching them with his left arm extended forward holding a lantern. In his right hand was a machete and on his left hip was a holstered Desert Eagle.

"Nathan," Kyle said, "what makes you think this hell hole will be any different than any other place?"

6

Nathan grinned. His teeth shone a pearly white, illuminated by the soft glow of his lantern. "Because, my friend of oh-so-little faith, this place isn't on any map I have. You know what that means?"

"You need to look for maps in places other than gas stations."

"No, it means this place is chock full of top secret, high-class technology."

"Sometimes, Nathan, I think you're chock full of bullshit."

"Just you wait. We're going to replace that antique of yours with a laser blaster or something."

Kyle put his hand over his gun. "I'll have you know that I like my antique," he snapped.

"Fine, then! I'll keep the laser blaster!"

Layla cut in, rolling her eyes. "I think you've been watching my sci-fi movies too much. It's highly unlikely they exist in any usable, let alone practical, form."

Nathan stomped his right foot, sending tremors throughout the surrounding area. "Unlikely doesn't mean impossible, damn it! You two have absolutely no vision whatsoever!"

Their bickering was cut short by a crackling static from Nathan's coat pocket.

Bzzzt "Nathan, this is Erin. Do you copy?" *Bzzzt*

Nathan reached inside his coat and pulled out a small disc with a green button on the side. Nathan pushed the button and spoke with his mouth against the disc.

"Yeah, Erin, I read you," he said calmly, trying to mask his irritation with Kyle and Layla, "what's up?"

Bzzzt "I think I've found something. Looks like it used to be a high-security room. The circuits are dead, obviously, but the door is frozen shut." *Bzzzt*

Nathan's face began to light up again. He faced his friends and grinned like a small child. "What did I tell you, guys? I knew this place was gold!" Nathan pressed the green button again. "Where are you, Erin?"

Bzzzt "Follow the north corridor back to the elevator shafts. Climb down the left shaft and head straight. You'll see me next to the door." *Bzzzt*

"We're on our way. Hang tight. Nathan, out." Nathan pocketed the disc and smiled once more at his friends. "Let's go! We've got a treasure chest to crack!"

* * *

Sitting in the dark, only a dim glow of a dying flare to keep the shadows at bay, sat a young woman. Her wild, fiery red hair concealed her sharp, green eyes. Her arms squeezed at her own body, listening, praying. The crucifix that dangled from her neck, barely visible beneath her red jumpsuit, gave her comfort in this dreary place. Her faith, which the others only laughed at, gave her comfort, for it was the only source of hope she knew in this cold, cruel world.

"Mama," the woman whispered, "why did you have to leave me?" Her head sank into her lap. "Why, God? God, why did you have to take her? It's not fair."

Footsteps echoed from down the corridor and she slowly rose to her feet. Almost instinctively, she rested her left hand on her hip, which a black, cloth belt clung to, and raised her right hand in front of her defensively. A faint glow grew into an overwhelming aurora, as three figures appeared out of the darkness.

The woman dropped her right hand in front of her and bowed. "Glad you could join me," she said with a sly grin. "Did you big, strong men come to help poor, weak Erin open this door?"

"Cute," Kyle said, completely deadpan and straight faced. He pulled a small, black orb from a pocket in his armor and placed it along the edge of the door. "Big, strong Kyle is gonna make a big, loud boom, so if you would be so kind, please get the hell out of the way."

Everyone did so as Kyle unholstered his pistol and slowly took twenty paces from the door, counting off each one. "About face." He turned and faced the door. "Aim." He armed for the orb. "Fire."

Bang

A deafening explosion rocked the corridor as Kyle's bullet came into contact with the black orb. After a minute, the smoke cleared and the door that had once stood in the gang's way was no more.

"You like that, Nathan?" Kyle said, rather proud of himself. "Pretty fucking good for some antiques." He turned and walked through the hole he had created. "Who needs your damn laser blasters? My flintlock pistol and my gunpowder cotton do the job just right." He turned to face his friends. "Speed and brains: that's what gets the job d-"

Kyle was cut off abruptly as Nathan pushed past him to examine the room. Like a child who didn't get the present he was hoping for at Christmas, Nathan's face fell.

"Empty?" he said. "Fucking...empty?"

"Aw, damn it!" Kyle yelled as he punched the wall. "Another fucking wild goose chase!"

"Wait," Layla cut in, pushing past Kyle and Nathan. "What's that?" Layla pointed to a pillar in the center of the barren room, covered by what appeared to be a very thick tarp.

"Well, Nathan, this is your treasure," Erin chimed in, "go pull that tarp off and see what you've found."

Slowly, Nathan approached the pillar, reaching for the tarp, when suddenly he stopped, frozen in place.

"Nathan?" Kyle asked, actually somewhat concerned. "What's up?"

"It's…humming," Nathan replied.

"What?" Erin and Layla both exclaimed in unison.

"Yeah," Nathan said, "it's humming…" He grabbed the tarp before anyone could say anything else and pulled it off.

"My God…" Erin whispered.

Before them all was a glass container, filled with a light-blue liquid. Floating in the liquid was a young man in a blue and white jumpsuit. Tubes came from the glowing base of the container, each attached to different joint of the suit. A mask covered the man's face, only his eyes exposed to the liquid. His brown hair floated like seaweed inside the container, his limbs dangling like those of a rag doll.

"What…" Kyle whispered, "…the fuck is that?"

"It… it just can't be…" Layla stammered. "A… person?"

"How can there still be power here?" Nathan said, to no one in particular.

10

"Fuck the power, man!" Kyle said, throwing his arms in the air. "There's a person in there!"

"No... no way. It's not possible." Nathan took a step forward, and suddenly the liquid illuminated and bubbles began to fill the container. "Oh, hell..."

The tubes began to rattle wildly within the container, which had begun to crack. The four backed away from the container as it continued to crack and fill with more bubbles. Finally, the container shattered and the liquid flooded out onto the floor. Lying in the center of the room was the man, the tubes and mask now gone. Slowly, the four approached the body, weapons, or fists in Erin's case, drawn and at the ready.

"Is it alive?" Erin asked.

Suddenly, the body twitched and coughed, then laid still for a time. Its eyelids slowly opened, revealing brilliant-green eyes. Then, in the voice of an angel, it spoke.

"I am awake."

Chapter II

No one knew what to make of the situation. It shouldn't have even been possible. Yet there they were, standing around a strange man lying in a pool of a glowing, blue liquid. Slowly, the man rose to his feet, as did the surrounding four's weapons.

"Where am I?" the strange man asked. He slowly turned in a complete circle, his eyes tracing every detail of the one standing directly in front of him. Finally, he stopped in front of Erin. "Do you know where I am?"

Erin was silent. The answer was no, but she simply couldn't form the response. No one bothered to answer the question for her, so they stood there for a great while, all five completely unsure of what to do.

"Maybe you do not know the answer," the strange man spoke again, still calm, his voice soothing. "I am sorry. I should not have assumed that you did. Let me ask another question." He waited, looking to see if there seemed to be an objection, which there wasn't. "Am I alive?"

"You... look alive," Layla stammered. She ran her eyes over the man's body, as he turned to meet her, finally meeting his eyes. "Are... are you human?"

"I do not know," the strange man replied.

"You... you don't know?" Kyle broke in, now very much more confused than he thought was possible. "What the hell are you?"

"I do not know." The strange man said this as he turned to face Kyle. Now looking into Kyle's eyes, the man continued. "I do not know who I am, what I am, where I am, or how I came to be." He leaned forward. "Do you know where I am?"

"No, I don't. None of us do. I don't want to know where I am. I don't even want to know what, who, or where you are either. I just want to know the way out of this shit hole!"

"Kyle!" Nathan snapped. "Fucking chill out, would you? This is some major-league shit, right here." Nathan glared at his friend and looked back at the strange man. I really wish we could've just found laser blasters, he thought.

"What are laser blasters?" the strange man asked.

Nathan froze. "What the hell did you just say?"

"I asked you 'what are laser blasters.' Just a moment ago, you stopped speaking by moving your mouth and said, 'I really wish we could've just found laser blasters.' What are laser blasters?"

"You…" Nathan didn't know what to say or do. He was living in one of Layla's sci-fi movies. "You're a telepath?"

"What is a telepath?"

"Someone who can read minds, hear thoughts."

"Perhaps. I do not know." He blinked and tilted his head. "What is a laser blaster?"

"It's a weapon. It shoots burning light."

"Why would you want such a thing?"

"Nathan!" Kyle shouted, clearly agitated. "Would you quit playing with the little doll and let us leave?"

The strange man turned to face Kyle, his green eyes piercing Kyle's very soul. "Doll?" He looked down at his hands and then looked over the rest of his body. "I'm a… doll?"

"No!" Erin had been silent and still up to this point. Her sudden outburst caught everyone off guard. "You're not a doll! You're a person and everything is going to be all right!" Erin's eyes glowed with a strange look of happiness as the strange man turned to face her. "We'll be your friends."

"Friend?" The man looked confused.

"It's someone you can trust. Someone who can trust you. A mutual guardian from everything bad in the world." Erin's face was brimming with a bizarre happiness, one her friends had no clue as to where it was coming from.

The strange man, for the first time, smiled. "Friend..." The man closed his eyes for a moment and then opened them. "I have friends. What do I call my friends?"

"My name is Erin." Erin bowed politely.

"My name is Nathan." Nathan seemed pleased to have made friends with the strange man, despite his earlier scare.

"You can call me Layla." Layla made a slight curtsy.

The strange man turned to them all, smiling as they said their names. He then turned to face Kyle and awaited his response. "What would this friend be called?"

My name is Kyle, Kyle thought.

The strange man smiled. "Friends. Erin, Nathan, Layla and Kyle are my friends." His face seemed to suddenly lose its glow and his smile began to fade. "I do not have a name."

"You don't know your name?" Erin asked.

"No. I do not know who, what, or where I am, nor do I know how I came to be."

"Well, maybe we could give you a name." Erin leaned forward, her eyes still aglow with the bizarre happiness. "Would you like that?"

The smile began to return to the strange man's face. "Yes, I would."

"All right!" Erin clapped her hands together and began to think of a name for the strange man. Before she had a chance, however, she was distracted by the clicking sound of guns. The five turned to face the sound and were greeted with the sight of two men, each holding a rusty hunting rifle, aimed to unleash a wave of bullets upon them.

"Abso-fucking-lutely touching, don't you think, Dan?" the man on the left bellowed. He was a giant, easily seven feet tall. His muscles rippled out of his jacket, and his scarred face was all the proof needed to know he was crazy. "Too bad the doll has to die along with his new friends."

At the sound of the giant's words, the strange man's eyes widened and a fire was sparked within them. He began to walk forward, past his new friends and straight towards the offenders. "You will not hurt my friends." His eyes hardened into an icy glare, his green eyes no longer peaceful, but menacing. Then, in a voice like a demon, he spoke again. "Should you try, I will break you."

"Wrong, asshole," the man on the right, Dan, said. His blonde, shaggy hair hid his eyes, making only his wicked grin visible. "Jack and I are gonna break you!" With that, he fired at the strange man. The bullet pierced the air, hurdling forward with speed that the human eye could never hope to detect. Finally, the bullet made contact.

Ping

The bullet bounced off the ground, rolling harmlessly away from the steel wall it had struck.

"You missed." The strange man looked directly into his would-be killer's eyes. Before there was time to react, the rifle was pried from

Dan's hands, and a bullet was delivered to his brain, via his left nostril.

"Holy shit!" Jack bellowed. "You mother fucker!" He rotated his hips, preparing to aim at the strange man, but before he could line up the rifle, it had been blocked by the rifle in the strange man's hands.

"Oh my God," Erin whispered.

"Christ, Nathan," Kyle muttered, "what did you find?"

"What the hell are you?" Jack grunted, struggling with all his might to break the strange man's guard.

The strange man's eyes burned with hatred, yet his toned could not have been colder. "Your worst nightmare." The strange man swept his leg behind Jack's and sent him toppling over backwards. The strange man's fist fell upon the defenseless giant's throat, and before any could make a sound, Jack's neck was crushed to a bloody pulp.

Nathan was speechless.

Kyle was speechless.

Layla was speechless.

Erin was frozen.

Silently, the four friends watched as the strange man slowly rose to his feet and then turned to face them. His eyes had returned to normal, and his face was calm. "My friends are now safe." His voice had also returned to its original, angelic tone. The strange man smiled warmly, his hand dripping Jack's blood. "Have you thought of a name for me?"

16

Chapter III

It had been a full day since they had returned from the science facility, yet Erin could still not think of a name for the strange man that had both mesmerized and horrified her. The thought had weighed heavily on her mind ever since they had found him, but she still wasn't even certain why. When she first laid eyes on him, he was an innocent angel. But the second an enemy appeared, he became a ruthless killer. Why am I so fascinated by him, she wondered.

"You do not have to think on it so hard, Erin," the strange man said, towering over her as she laid in her bed.

"Jesus!" she shrieked, curling into a ball and pulling the sheets over her body. "What the hell are you doing in here?"

"I'm sorry. I did not mean to scare you. I heard you whispering as I sat outside your door."

"I wasn't whispering, I was thinking! Keep your telepathy in check, would you? A woman's mind is not something a man should pry into!"

"I'm sorry. I do not know how to stop it. I can close my eyes and cover my ears. I can hold my nose and shut my mouth. But I cannot stop myself from sensing the thoughts of others, much like I cannot numb my touch or dull my taste. I'm sorry, but I cannot control it."

"Then just don't tell us about it. Ignorance is bliss."

"All right."

There was an awkward silence. "You can leave now," she said, softly.

"All right. Good bye, Erin." The strange man turned and walked out of Erin's room, taking a glance over his shoulder before moving out of sight.

Erin let out a long sigh and stared at the ceiling, her eyes piercing the concrete and gazing into space. What do I call you, she wondered.

* * *

What will she call me, the strange man wondered. No past, no name, no explanation... what am I?

You are what you perceive yourself to be.

The strange man froze immediately. He stared straight ahead, focusing on nothing, his body a statue. You, he thought. Who are you?

I've told you already.

I don't understand.

That is expected. How are you feeling?

Lost. Confused.

Are you scared?

No.

You should be.

Why?

Do you remember your father?

No. Is that what I should be afraid of?

Yes.

Why?

Your soul is tainted.

My soul?

Try to remember.

I can't remember anything.

You must.

How?

Pray.

What?

Ask Erin. She will guide you.

Yes, I believe you. Erin is my friend.

"Adam!" Erin cried out from behind him.

The strange man turned to face her. Her hair was pulled back into a neat ponytail, allowing him a clear view of the green eyes that had been hidden when they first met. "Excuse me?" he said, caught suddenly off his guard.

"That'll be your name: Adam!"

The strange man closed his eyes and absorbed her words. After a short while, the strange man opened his eyes and smiled. "My name is Adam," he said warmly. "It is a good name."

Erin squealed with delight. "You like it?" She clasped her hands together and a bright smile spread across her face.

Adam nodded. "Yes. I like it very much."

"I'm so happy!" She laughed and brought up her hands to cover her mouth, trying not to look so immature. The truth of the matter, strangely enough, was that she really didn't care. For some reason unknown to her, this man, Adam, made her feel happy, made her feel safe.

"Adam, huh?" Kyle called from down the corridor, slowly making his way towards the two. "How do you like that for a name, doll?"

"Kyle!" Erin snapped, putting her hands on her hips. "Don't call him that! He's a person, just like you and me!"

"Uh-huh, yeah," Kyle said with a smirk, "whatever you say, Erin."

"Kyle, why do you have to be such a jerk?"

"Jerk?" Adam broke in. "What is a jerk?"

"Someone who's mean for the fun of it." Erin glared at Kyle, like he was a dog that just urinated in its master's shoe.

"Erin," Kyle sighed, "you make it out like I intend to be a dickhead."

"Dickhead?" Adam asked again.

"A big jerk," Kyle answered.

"You do, though!" Erin continued. "You could at least be polite to Adam, if no one else!"

"Wait, is Kyle a jerk or a dickhead?"

"Hey, I don't have to baby sit Nathan's treasure! I can be as much of an asshole as I want!"

"Kyle, you are biggest baby I've ever had the misfortune of knowing!"

"Asshole?" Adam was thoroughly confused at this point.

"Don't make it sound like you're the only one that suffers in this little relationship!"

"You wish we had a relationship, you bastard!"

"Kyle is many things."

"Yeah, like I wish I had colon cancer!"

"You conceited, wretched prick!"

"Prick what?"

"Erin, you're breaking my heart."

"I'll break your neck!"

Touch her shoulder.

Adam froze. The voice from within was calling to him once again.

Touch her shoulder, now.

Why?

Trust me.

Adam obeyed and placed his hand on Erin's shoulder. Instantly, he felt her body shiver and felt her very anger and frustration melt away. He watched her face lose its hard edge, and a peaceful glaze came over her eyes. Finally, she looked into Kyle's eyes and smiled. "It's late," she said, "I'm going to bed now. Goodnight, Kyle! Goodnight, Adam!" She turned to go back into her room, but then spun back around and wrapped her arms

20

around Adam. Again, he was able to feel her emotion, but this time he felt the warm embrace of her joy. She smiled and retreated to her room and collapsed on her bed.

"Fucking doll," Kyle murmured, and he too turned and walked away.

Adam stood in the corridor waiting for Kyle to disappear from sight. "Doll? Am I a doll?"

"Nah, you're not a doll," a voice called from the shadows. "Kyle just likes confrontation." The voice slowly came into the dim light and Adam smiled.

"Hello, Nathan," Adam said cheerfully. Nathan was the friend who seemed to be the most interested in him, save for possibly Erin.

"Hey. Erin give you a name yet?"

"Yes. My name is Adam."

"Adam, huh? That's a good, solid name. You like it?"

"Yes, I do."

"Good to hear." He offered a friendly smiled and put his hand on Adam's shoulder. Like with Erin, Adam could sense Nathan's emotions. However, Nathan's emotions remained constant, unlike with Erin.

"So, how you like our little hideout?"

"It's…" Adam paused for a moment, considering his response. "…cold."

Nathan continued to smile, but his lips closed, hiding his teeth. "Yeah, that it is. But most places are cold, sadly. It could be worse, though. That place where we found you was freezing!"

"Yes, you are right." Adam looked down at the ground for a moment and then looked back up at Nathan. "Nathan?"

"Yeah, buddy?"

"No, my name is Adam."

Nathan let out a light chuckle. "No, no, I know what your name is. Buddy is another word for friend."

"Oh. I understand."

"So, what were you going to ask me?"

"What am I?"

Nathan's smiled faded. "I don't know, Adam." He closed his eyes for a second and then opened them, sighing. "Near as I can tell, you're an abandoned science experiment."

"Why would someone abandon me?"

Nathan's face seemed sad suddenly. He swallowed hard. "Adam, I think it's time someone told you why there are no warm places anymore, why the world is covered in snow and ice and why in your first moments awake you were exposed to violence."

Adam leaned his back against the wall. "Tell me. I'm listening."

* * *

It was a time of technological prosperity. Almost everyday, a new scientist emerged from the headlines with a new invention. The natures of the inventions of that era are now irrelevant. All except one.

It was a machine that could create extreme temperatures in the form of a beam. The idea behind it was to create cooling beams to counteract global warming and to prevent polar ice caps from melting. It was a great idea for a great invention. However, a group of terrorists saw it as a means for personal gain.

The terrorists killed the creators of the machine, as well as those who protected it, cleaned it and even looked at it. They were the standard terrorists of the time: demanding, ruthless and utterly stupid. They moved the machine to some remote base in a location that no longer matters. They demanded large amounts of money, land and a litany of other ridiculous things. Naturally, their demands were rejected, so they prepared to use the machine.

Not only did they manage to cause the machine to overload and fire a beam measuring absolute zero, they hit dead on at the center of the North Pole. It can't be stressed how fast the planet entered an ice age.

After years of hiding, the climate grew tolerable enough for people to return to the surface. But those that did quickly learned that surviving in this new word meant forsaking their humanity and becoming murdering scavengers. Clans, tribes and gangs were formed and the people began the endless hunt for food, medicine and technology of any kind, and so a brave, new world was born.

* * *

Adam didn't move or speak. He couldn't. What awful world had he been born into? Deep down, he felt something burn inside of him: something dark, something terrible. It was the same feeling that had overwhelmed him when he killed those two men. His friends, such good friends, his guardians, his trustees, those that saved him from the cold and from absolute uncertainty, had been cursed to live in this cruel world, as well.

"Adam," Nathan said, "are you all right?"

Now you know exactly where you are.

I don't want to be here.

Do you think your friends are any different?

Can I help them?

Yes.

How?

When you accept what you are, you will know.

What am I?

Part II: Wings of an Angel

Chapter IV

Adam wasn't particularly sure of what to make of the spikes protruding from the middle of his back. It had begun with a mild itching sensation, one that slowly covered all of his back. Then the pain: the maddening, pin-point pressure pain in his spine. After about a day or so, the pain had centralized to the location of two large bumps on the center of his back, one on each side of his spine. Another day passed, and the bumps were replaced with short, black, curved spikes which pointed upward, making leaning his back against anything quite painful. Normally, anything that crossed his mind he could tell Erin. But not this, for something made him reluctant, and because he didn't know what that something was, it made him angry.

Adam rose from his seat and carefully donned the fur coat that Nathan had given to him. He always wore it outside of his room, which was more of a closet than a room, because the spikes had already torn through his jumpsuit. Nathan had offered to get him an entirely new outfit, but Adam politely turned down the offer and accepted the fur coat, but only after three days of constant nagging, as well as the realization that the jumpsuit would not hide the spikes for long. Secure in the belief that he had hidden the spikes beneath his coat, he walked out of his room and headed for the kitchen, which was on the opposite end of the hideout.

* * *

"What a shit hole," Kyle murmured as he stumbled into the kitchen, just as the light bulb exploded. Glass showered down upon the table in the center of the room, several pieces finding their way into Nathan's cereal.

"Kyle," Nathan mumbled, half-awake, "if you could find 12-watt bulbs instead of 8-watt bulbs, they would just burn out instead of exploding onto my cereal."

"I told you already, asshole! The 12-watts cost a fortune! Maybe if we'd find something useful on one of your little camping trips, I could have something to trade besides copper wiring!"

"That copper wiring was found on one of my 'little camping trips,' and has lasted us for about two months as a solid trade good."

"We're almost out of it. I give it one more trip into town."

"Kyle, have I ever told you that you are a very pessimistic person?"

"No, tell me."

"You're a very pessimistic person."

"Thanks for letting me know." Kyle opened the cupboard and opened a box of light bulbs. He took one out and replaced the ruined bulb. Immediately, the room was filled with light once more, revealing to plain sight the ugly, peeling wall paper.

"What a shit hole," Layla commented as she walked into the kitchen. She walked over to the cupboard that Kyle had procured the light bulbs from and pulled out a bag of very stale pretzels.

Nathan shook his head and went back to picking glass shards out of his cereal. "Are you two ever happy?"

"Sure," Kyle said, plucking a pretzel out of the bag in Layla's hands, "when I'm eating."

"I'm happy," Layla said, "whenever I'm fighting."

Nathan raised an eyebrow. "Fighting?"

"Yeah! Proving I'm alive, tasting the blood of my enemies on my katanas, seeing the fear in the eyes of grown men when they see my shotgun aimed at their chests! The adrenaline, the sweat, the blood: it's absolutely maddening!" She seemed to be getting a high just talking about it. "I love it."

"Layla, you need help."

"Can I help?" Adam said softly as he walked into the room.

"Oh, for fuck's sake," Kyle mumbled, "what the hell is wrong with you?"

"Nothing. I just thought I heard Nathan say that Layla needed help."

Nathan and Layla just laughed. "No, she's all right, Adam," Nathan chuckled. "I'm just teasing her, that's all."

"Oh, I understand."

Adam's attention turned to the light bulb dangling from the ceiling. It was small and looked like it had been forced into the socket. "Excuse me," he said, "how is that working without..." Adam paused for a minute. "Power? Is that what you called it, Nathan?"

Nathan looked up at the bulb. "Oh yeah, that's my contribution to this humble abode."

"I'm not sure I'd call that leaky, tangled mess you call a generator a contribution, Nathan," Kyle said, looking up at the light bulb.

"I'm not sure I'd use the word humble to describe this place, either," Layla added.

Adam looked at Nathan and smiled. "You've made something good in a bad world. That's worthy of praise, Nathan."

Nathan grinned and turned to Layla and Kyle. "Hear that? It's worthy of praise!"

28

Kyle stared blankly at Adam and just shook his head. "Fucking doll."

"Kyle!" Layla yelled, smacking Kyle in the chest. "Can't you at least pretend to be polite?"

"When am I ever polite?"

"The key word was pretend, Kyle."

Before an argument could ensue, Erin walked into the room and stood next to Adam, rubbing her eyes. "What's all the fuss about?"

Nathan didn't bother to look up from his bowl of cereal and glass chips. "Kyle's ripping on Adam, again."

"Kyle!" Erin shouted, glaring harshly at him. "Why do you have to be so mean to Adam? He never did anything to you!"

"Whatever," Kyle murmured, averting his eyes from Erin's.

"No!" Erin smashed her fist against the door frame and stormed over to Kyle, grabbed the collar of his jacket and pulled him and inch from her face. "Don't you 'whatever' me! Adam has been here for a week and everyone but you had had no problem accepting him! What's your problem?"

"What's your problem?" Kyle snapped back. "Ever since we found this guy, you've been acting like he's your baby brother. So what if I'm rude to him? I'm rude to everyone! Why should I suddenly be polite to some doll we found in a jar?"

Erin balled her fist and gritted her teeth. She instantly relaxed, however, as Adam's hand clasped around her wrist. Slowly, her anger and frustration began to melt and was replaced by a calming sense of peace.

"Please, friends," Adam said softly, "don't fight."

Free from Erin's grip, Kyle stormed out of the room. Nathan and Layla remained still, watching as Erin's expression lost its hard edge. Slowly, Adam released Erin's wrist and pulled out a seat at the table for Erin to sit down. Once she was situated, Adam took a seat next to her and Nathan and turned to look to Layla.

"Won't you sit down, Layla?" Adam said with a smile.

Layla shook her head with a grin. "Amazing," she said with a light chuckle. "How anyone can be so calm and level headed in this place is simply amazing. Oh, what the hell." Layla walked over to the table and sat down next to Erin. "You found a real gem, Nathan. I think Adam beats a laser blaster, don't you?"

Nathan pushed his bowl away, convinced he'd never remove all the glass from his cereal. "Damn right, I did!" Nathan patted Adam on the shoulder and smiled. "Best thing I've ever found."

Adam felt a surge of pride flowing through his body, springing forth from Nathan's hand. Strange, he thought, that I can make Erin's emotions turn to joy, but I have no effect on Nathan.

"So," Layla said while tapping the table with her palms, "what's the next treasure site going to be?"

Nathan pulled out a map, unfolded it and laid it out on the table. "We're going back to where we found Adam."

"What? Nathan, there's nothing there!"

"There's power there."

"What are you talking about, Nathan?" Erin said, finally waking up from her joyous daze.

"When we found Adam, that spot was definitely receiving power from something. I want to find out what."

"Nathan," Layla said sternly, "you're our leader, and I'll go wherever you think we should go. But that place..." She paused and took a deep breath. "That place... it's dangerous."

"Dangerous? The whole damn world is dangerous! Wha-"

Layla cut him off. "Listen to me. I've killed a lot of people, I've seen some terrible things and I've committed some equally terrible acts. I'm a dangerous person, Nathan." She looked hard into Nathan's eyes. "And that place scares me."

"Then you can stay behind. Erin, Adam and I will go back."

"Wait, you're taking Adam?" Erin blurted. "What about Kyle? Where's he fit in?"

"Kyle will be taking the last of the copper wiring and the weapons and supplies we found on those two raiders into town to trade."

"But, why Adam?"

"Why not? He killed two fully armed men that were twice his size without even getting flushed."

"But-"

Nathan held up his hand. "But nothing! Adam is a powerful asset to this gang. Not only that, but it's possible he might even learn something about himself down there." He turned to Adam. "Unless you have qualms about go-"

"No," Adam said firmly, "I want to go."

"Then it's settled." Nathan stood up and walked towards the door on the left side of the room, which lead to his, Erin's and Adam's rooms. "We leave tomorrow at dawn."

Adam watched Nathan walk out of sight and then turned to Erin and Layla. "Should I be opposed to his?"

"It's your call, Adam," Erin said quietly. "I just thought you'd be reluctant to go back to that place."

"I will go wherever Nathan wants me to go. I trust him."

"You've only known us for a week, though!"

"You are my friends. I trust you."

Erin smiled. "I wish I had that kind of faith in people."

"I don't understand," Adam tilted his head. "Why is it so desirable?"

"When you're wary of others' motives, you're never able to relax."

"Are you able to relax around me?"

Erin's smiled widened and she nodded. "Yes, I am."

"You have only known me for a week."

"You're my friend. I trust you."

There was a peaceful silence between the two for some time, long enough to bore Layla and force her out the door to her room. Once Layla was beyond earshot, Adam broke the silence.

"Erin," Adam whispered, "may I ask you a favor?"

"Of course!" Erin replied. "What is it?"

"Can you teach me how to pray?"

Erin's face lit up. "Of course I can!" She closed her eyes and took a deep breath. "All right, first clear your head. Next, close your eyes and fold your hands." Erin and Adam both closed their eyes and folded their hands. "Now, simply form your thoughts and lay them out before God. Simple!"

Adam was about to ask how one laid something before God, whoever that was, when suddenly felt a crawling sensation in the back of his skull. For the first time since he awoke in that cold room, something was familiar.

Go on. Pray.

Who is God?

Pray and you will remember.

Form thoughts, Adam thought. What thought do I give to God?

Adam searched the corridors of his mind, desperately filtering through the sea of thoughts that had overwhelmed him in the past week. Yet, amidst all the chaos, confusion, anger, happiness and sorrow, Adam could only form a single thought.

What am I?

In the instant Adam posed the question, a searing pain pierced his heart and Adam screamed in agony as he collapsed to the ground. Nothing but pain registered to Adam's senses. Then, the pain ceased, and an enormous voice echoed in his mind.

WHO ARE YOU, TAINTED ONE?

Again, Adam's body swelled with pain and nothing else could be felt. The pain faded one more and the voice spoke again.

WINGS OF AN ANGEL, BLOOD OF A DEMON. YOU ARE AN ABOMINATION!

Adam suddenly felt a great sense of despair overcome him. It was a feeling more horrible than the overwhelming pain of a moment ago. Adam's eyes swelled with tears as he formed the name of the dread emotion.

Rejection.

Chapter V

Adam had wanted so badly to know what he was, but now he was sorry he had ever concerned himself with the question. He never wanted to feel so sad, so hurt ever again. Lying on the ground, staring up at the ceiling, his friends huddled around him, their thoughts swirling incoherently in his head.

Is he alive?

What the hell happened?

Please, God, don't let him leave me.

Fucking doll.

Why is his back arched?

Are those feathers?

You can't be serious.

Wings?

Adam closed his eyes and slowly sat up, his back throbbing in pain. He raised his right eyebrow as he felt a new sensation, as if arms were coming from his back. He turned his head and opened his eyes and was astonished at the spectacle: small, black wings.

"Erin," Nathan said, his voice trying to be firm, but was still noticeably shaken, "what happened?"

"Adam asked me to teach him how to pray," Erin replied, incredibly shaken, "and then he started screaming!"

"I always knew that religious shit was bad news," Kyle groaned.

"Shut up, Kyle!"

"Cut it out, both of you!" Nathan shouted. He knelt down next to Adam and rested his hand on Adam's shoulder. "Hey man. Can you stand up?"

Adam shook violently, resenting Nathan's touch. "Don't touch me!" he screamed, wrapping his arms around his body, holding himself in a ball. "Don't... touch me."

Nathan jumped back, caught completely off guard by Adam's out-of-character outburst. "Damn, man," Nathan stammered as he watched Adam's body shake like a cold, shivering child.

"I... I'm sorry. I just..." Adam closed his eyes and thought hard on the emotion he was feeling. "I'm scared."

"Aw," Kyle said mockingly, "the doll is scared."

Adam abruptly shot up to his feet. His arms shot out and slammed Kyle against the wall, the plaster cracking from the impact. "I'm not a doll!" Adam screamed. "I am flesh and bone and blood! I think! I feel! I'm not a doll!" Adam clenched his teeth as Kyle's emotions flooded his senses. Surprise. Anger. Resentment. Fear. Anger.

Anger.

Anger.

"You... monster." Adam glared at Kyle with an expression colder than where he had been found, his eyes filled with some unearthly flame. Then, in an instant, it was gone, replaced by a lost stare. He loosened his grip and took two steps backwards, slowly lowering his head, averting his eyes from Kyle and the others. "I'm... sorry."

* * *

Wings, Adam thought. Black wings, like those of a crow. Where did they come from? Why did they appear? What am I?

You are what you perceive yourself to be.

What does that mean?

What do you think it means?

35

What I think I am is what I am?
…*No.*
What then?
You can't simply think. You must believe.
Believe what?
"Adam?"

Adam looked up from the floor of his room. "Oh, hello, Erin," Adam said softly. His voice had a hint of regret in it, still pained by his actions that morning. "Are… you mad at me?"

"Of course not!" Erin plopped down next to Adam on the floor, quickly glancing at his wings. "Kyle got what he deserved. It's just…" Erin took a deep breath. "We would've never expected it to come from you."

"I never would've expected it, either," Adam said, now speaking just above a whisper. "Erin, what's wrong with me?"

"Nothing, Adam!" She placed her hand on his. "You woke up in a cold, ruined science facility and were forced to kill in your first moments awake. Not to mention that you were found by us, of all people, and now you're living with us!" She tensed her face, as if trying to hide some deeper concern. "Adam, nothing is wrong with you."

"Then why do I have black wings as a result of praying?" Adam pulled his hand away from Erin and looked back at the floor. "Why can I hear people's thoughts and feel their emotions? Why…" Adam stopped himself before he could mention the voices. Somehow he knew that hearing voices was something even Erin would think strange. "Why?"

Erin folded her hands in her lap and joined Adam in staring at the floor. After some time, she closed her eyes and laid her head upon Adam's shoulder. "I don't care."

Adam darted his eyes towards Erin. "What?"

"I don't care if you can read my mind or feel what I'm feeling. I don't care if wings are sprouting from your back." Erin cracked a smile. "All I care about is how happy I feel when you hold me, even if it's only for an instant." Erin sat back up and stared at the ceiling. "It's late. I'm going to bed." Erin stood up and smiled at Adam, resting her hand against his cheek. "Goodnight, Adam."

"Goodnight."

Erin, Adam thought, why do you care about me?"

She accepts you the way you are.

You make it seem like that's special.

Kyle hates you. Layla is apathetic towards you. Nathan is intrigued only by your potential. Erin cares about you for no reason other than you are yourself.

Who are you?

I told you.

You said you were me.

The old you.

What was that?

I cannot tell you.

Why?

You are not ready.

When will that be?

When your father speaks to you again.

Chapter VI

Dawn had come at last to the frozen wastes, the world illuminated by the light reflected from thick layers of snow. Emerging from the frozen remains of a bar, two men and a woman began to forge through the snow and ice.

* * *

"Erin," Nathan said, "you've been awfully quiet this morning. You all right?"

"Yeah," Erin replied, "just weird not having Kyle and Layla along."

"Yeah, I know. Who would've thought I'd miss that bastard's yap." Nathan turned to look at Adam. "How about you, buddy? Miss ol' Kyle's-"

"No," Adam said sharply. He didn't even bother to look at Nathan when he responded. Something didn't feel right this morning. Something, Adam thought, is terribly wrong.

* * *

"Layla," Kyle mumbled, "I'm headed for town to trade what junk we have left. You want anything in particular?"

"No," Layla responded as she gnawed on some beef jerky, "I'm fine."

"All right, hold the fort down." Kyle turned and headed down the right hallway and headed for the stairwell to the surface. For some reason, he felt wrong about leaving Layla alone, as if she were in danger. That was, of course, absurd, as nothing was a threat to Layla.

* * *

The group trudged on, carrying their weapons with a bizarre pride. The icy wind that whipped at their faces failed to deter them from their destination. Off in the distance, a ruined apartment building towered menacingly above streets of frozen wreckage. Cars lay strewn across their path, embedded in layers upon layers of ice. The group arrived outside of the apartment building and checked their weapons, then stormed inside.

* * *

"So," Erin said, "here we are… again." Erin carefully slid through the hole in the fence that Kyle had created on the previous visit. "I can't blame Layla for not wanting to come back here. This place is… scary."

"Erin," Nathan groaned, "you and Layla have been acting pretty girly as of late. I'm really disappointed. What happened to my two fearless women?"

"Just because Kyle isn't here, doesn't mean you have to be a jerk to pick up the slack." She grinned. "Besides, you're bad at it."

Adam looked inside of the facility and closed his eyes. "This place," he said, "sickens me."

* * *

Kyle jogged through the snow and skidded across sheet after sheet of ice. He held his pistol tight in his right hand, his eyes darting back and forth across the surrounding area, as if he were being watched. Just as the thought had cross his mind, Kyle heard the crunching of snow behind him. He spun on a dime, his arm extended, ready to plant a bullet into the skull of his enemy.

* * *

The group split up, the woman moving down the stairwell while the men searched the first floor. There was nothing but broken, useless electronics and trash from what used to be a trashcan. In the basement, the woman slowly crept into what appeared to be a functional kitchen. The woman was not as fortunate as the men had been, however, for she had found herself on the receiving end of a shotgun and a wicked smile.

* * *

"All right," Nathan said, "we went down two floors to get to the room where we found Adam. I say we head down three and see what we find."

"Sounds like a plan to me," Erin replied. "Adam, you ready to move out?"

Adam rolled his head back ad closed his eyes, but did not respond.

"Buddy?" Nathan whispered, concerned about his friend's strange silence. "You okay?"

"Adam?" Erin said, moving close to him. "What is it?"

"Something's wrong…" Adam replied gravely.

* * *

"Sneaky mother fucker," Kyle cackled as he stood over the wounded boy. "Thought you'd try to jump me, did you?"

"No… sir," the boy groaned. He couldn't have been older than 15. His brown eyes were filled with horror and his blue and orange hair was drenched with sweat. Tears streamed down the boy's cheeks as he stared up at Kyle. "Please… I only wanted some food. Please, don't kill me… please!"

"Sorry, kid, but I hate beggars." Kyle's eyes were filled with a sickening delight as he towered over the boy, the barrel of his gun pointed between the boy's eyes.

* * *

40

The wicked smile had quickly faded to a blood stained grimace as bullets punctured the body it belonged to. The two men stood over their fallen comrade and her murderer, looked at each other and emptied the clips of their weapons into the body of that wicked smile. The two men reloaded, shrugged their shoulders and began to loot the building, starting with the two corpses at their feet.

* * *

Adam stumbled and collapsed to the ground, just outside of the glowing door. "Oh, no," he whispered in pain.

"Adam," Erin shrieked, "what's wrong?" She knelt down beside him, resting her hands on his right shoulder. "What is it?"

Nathan turned from the door and stamped his feet. "Come on, you two," he whined, "the answer to all the secrets of this place are sealed behind this door!" Nathan balled his hands into fists. "Adam, can't it wait?"

"Layla," Adam whispered,

* * *

Kyle's hand clenched his chest as he stumbled away from the bloody corpse. The pain was like nothing he had ever felt before, as if a thousand needles had been driven into his heart. He fell to his knees, dropping his pistol into the deep snow. The weight of his scythe now seemed unbearable, but it was nothing in comparison to this awful pain. "Something..." Kyle stammered, "something's happened... to my baby sister."

Chapter VII

"Layla?" Erin said, quizzically. "What about Layla?"

"She's… gone," Adam choked, his hands trembling. "I saw her… not her person, but a light… a thread. A blonde thread of hair… glowing, and then it… snapped. The light went away and the thread was soaked in blood." He looked up at Erin, his eyes letting forth a slow stream of tears. "Erin… Layla's dead."

Nathan, who had been acting like an impatient birthday boy until this point, stormed toward Adam, lifting up into the air by the collar of his jumpsuit. "The hell are you talking about?" he shouted. "Layla's the craziest bitch in the world and there's no way in hell she can be dead!" Nathan dropped Adam back to his feet and stormed towards the glowing door and smashed his fist against it. "Now, snap out of it and help me open this goddamn door!"

Adam slowly walked towards the door, his eyes fixed firmly on the ground. Layla, he thought, I'm so sorry. He looked up at the door, placing his hands against it, his fingers pressing down on it, adding more and more pressure each second. His mind flooded with memories of the past week, any thing that had to do with Layla. Then, Adam couldn't think of anything. Instead, he saw Dan and Jack, the two raiders he had killed the day he had awoke. They laughed hysterically, despite the bullet hole in Dan's head and Jack's smashed neck. The laughter echoed ceaselessly in his mind and their thought filled his ears, swirling into an incoherent mass.

You can't save them

You can't stop us.

You can't see us.

We are everywhere.

Doll.

The two men began to merge and blur, their voices becoming one.

What good is a doll?

Can't do anything that it isn't told to do.

No mind.

No heart.

No soul.

The blurring ceased and the voice was solid, and in an instant, Adam no longer saw Jack or Dan, but instead was looking at the grinning face of Kyle.

Just a fucking doll.

"NO!" Adam screamed, his pained voice shaking the very walls of the complex. "I'M NOT A DOLL!" Adam's muscles swelled and then tightened as his fingers crushed into the door, blood pouring from beneath his nails. His wings flapped furiously and his body crashed against the door, slowly crushing it as he screamed in fear, pain, sorrow, frustration and utter hatred. Adam fell forward, the door bursting forth from its frame and crashing to the cold, steel floor. Adam continued to clench the door, his tears mixing with his blood and sweat. "I'm not a doll, " he whispered. "I'm not a doll."

Nathan walked right past Adam into the room, just as he done to Kyle when they had found Adam. This time, however, Nathan was not disappointed whatsoever. Nathan found himself surrounded by flashing lights, glowing screens, cabinets full of tools and books and an enormous pillar of red-orange light. Nathan was in heaven.

Erin couldn't move. She didn't know which was more shocking: Nathan's complete lack of sympathy or Adam's outburst. Either way, she couldn't do anything to shake the spectacle from her mind. She simply stood there, frozen in time, replaying the event over and over again.

"This is amazing," Nathan said, astonished, "absolutely amazing!" Nathan spun around, his face brimming with joy and what seemed to be pride. "Adam, my friend, you just hit the jackpot! Just think: if Erin hadn't found the room you were sleeping in, we would have never found this place." Nathan turned back around, gazing at the pillar. "Amazing."

Adam exhaled slowly and closed his eyes. Pushing himself off the ground, he could hear Nathan's thoughts.

This is amazing. This is what I've always dreamed of finding. This definitely makes up for that last disappointment.

Adam opened his eyes, revealing the sadness that his eyelids had concealed. Disappointment, he thought. He walked over beside Nathan and joined him in staring blankly at the glowing pillar. "Find what you were looking for, Nathan?" he asked in a monotone voice.

"You bet, buddy! It's all thanks to you!" Nathan turned to Adam and patted him on the back. "Don't look so glum, Adam; this is a moment to be proud!"

"Yes," Adam said softly, shuffling his feet. He looked at his blood-stained hands and saw that the blood had stopped flowing from his nails. "What do you think this room is?"

Nathan walked around the room and noticed that against the back wall, behind the pillar, was a

44

large screen. Beneath the screen was a small terminal with a rather rickety-looking stool in front of it. "Well," Nathan said, rubbing his hands together, "let's see if we can find out!"

As Nathan walked towards the terminal, Erin slowly crept through the ruined door frame and stood next to Adam. "Are…" she whispered, "you all right?"

"I'm fine," Adam replied, still looking at his hands. "Nathan's finally found the treasure he's always wanted."

Erin glanced around the pillar to see Nathan typing away at the terminal. "It would seem that way." She looked down at the ground and sighed.

"Uh, Erin?" Nathan called. "Adam? You two might want to check this out!"

Adam and Erin looked up to see the screen lighting up, glowing a pale blue. Slowly, static began to fill the screen, and from it emerged an image of a city. Fire swept across the streets, children crying beneath the dead bodies of their parents. Gunshots rang out amidst the chaos, missiles steaming across the bloodshot sky, all aimed at some horrific figure in the distance.

"What on earth is this?" Erin asked.

Nathan looked down at the terminal and examined the caption next to the file. "Day of the Harbingers – 2033." Nathan looked back up at the screen. "Harbingers… what the hell?"

The chaos raged across the streets, the screen filling with more and more fire. The figure in the distance continued to walk forward, the fire and screaming seemingly dragged along. Slowly, just as the screams began to hurt the group's ears, the figure came into focus. A tall, muscular figure, with crimson red skin and giant, black bat wings from its back. Its jet black hair stood on end like cruel spikes, dark red streaks spread throughout the course mass. Two small horns, appearing razor sharp, protruded from the monster's forehead, one above each eye, and another curving out from its chin. It was grinning as it marched forward, bearing jagged, yellow teeth. But most horrifying of all was its brilliant, pupil less, yellow eyes.

"What the hell is that?" Nathan said, his voice filled with a mix of bewilderment, intrigue and fear.

Adam felt his blood boil within his veins, his muscles tightening subconsciously. Then, the crawling sensation returned, his mind swelling with a strange familiarity.

Volley after volley of bullets sped towards the figure, yet each bullet bounced harmlessly off the creature's wings. The missiles never came close to making contact, as if they were brushed aside by some unknown force.

"Wait," Erin said, equally bewildered as Nathan, "what's that light?"

In the sky above the demon, a faint white light was moving towards the figure at an alarming speed. The figure seemed to sense it and turned to meet the light, but the moment it had completed the turn, the light had struck the figure to the ground. The screen shook and crackled, but stayed in focus.

"Oh, my God," Erin whispered. "It can't be!"

"Holy shit!" Nathan shouted. "No way!"

Pinning the creature to the ground was a young man, his muscular body wrapped loosely in a white cloth, his figure encased in a brilliant white light. Sprouting from his back were two enormous, white wings, like those of a dove's. The man

46

looked forward, staring ahead at what was probably the camera that had filmed the event. His neatly groomed hair flowed as if it were in a cool breeze, his brilliant green eyes filled with a sense of great purpose. Staring forward, he raised his hand towards the screen. "This," he said, in the most melodic of voices, "was not meant for mortal eyes." A brilliant light filled the screen and then there was only static fuzz.

Adam stood frozen, his eyes wide with shock, staring silently up at the screen. Erin and Nathan both looked at each other and then stared at Adam.

"Is… Adam…" Nathan stammered.

Erin's breath was wild, her hands shaking as she opened her mouth. "An angel?"

Chapter VIII

The room suddenly felt colder to Adam, as if his clothes had been stripped from him and nothing stood between his skin and the icy chill of this wretched planet. He continued to stare up at the static fuzz on the screen, completely still. Erin and Nathan looked back to each other.

"No way," Nathan said, waving his arms in front of him as he took a step backwards. "That's just not fucking possible!"

"That was Adam on the screen!" Erin yelled, jabbing a finger towards the screen. "His eyes! His hair! His face! His voice!" She stomped her foot. "That was Adam! He had wings and was glowing white! How is that not possible?"

"'Cause angels don't exist, Erin!" He shook his head and pointed a finger at Erin. "It's not logical! God isn't logical and neither are angels! Whatever that thing was, it wasn't anything divine! It was probably some secret weapon that the old governments created and Adam is probably a left over replica or something like that!"

Erin grinded her teeth and then screamed. "What do you know? You don't know a damn thing, Nathan! Are you going to tell me that demonic monster was just some secret weapon, too? The future isn't one of Layla's sci-fi movies! It's me and you and Kyle and Layla and Adam! We're the future, not laser blasters and humanoid weapons!" Her eyes began to water and her bottom lip began to quiver. "Why is it so hard to have faith in something science can't prove? Why can't you see anything beyond your own logic? Why?" Erin clasped her right hand over her crucifix and stormed out the door, eyes fixed on the ground.

"Erin, come back! Damn it, Erin!" Nathan ran out after her, and Adam was left alone in the room.

Are you all right?

Am… I an angel?

To Erin, you are. To her, you are God's gift to this world.

I don't even know who God is.

You used to know.

What? When?

…

Talk to me! When did I know God?

…

Please! Say something!

…

Please…

How could you forget your own father?

A scream shook Adam awake. He spun around towards the door and ran outside of the room. Gunshots rang throughout the hall as Adam ran towards the screams. Adam paid no attention to where he was going; all he knew was that his friends needed him. Finally, he approached an empty hallway with a gaping hole in the wall ahead. Emanating from the hole was a neon green light, as well as the source of the noise. Adam ran forward and leapt through the hole in the wall, landing on a steel grate walkway. Ahead of him was a hardened and alert Erin, her body at an angle and her fists raised in front of her. At his feet was a bleeding, barely conscious Nathan. Behind him were three men with submachine guns.

"Adam!" Erin screamed, pointing behind him.

Adam spun around to see what she was pointing at, just in time to receive ten bullets in his chest. Three new faces stared at him, all possessing horrible grins. Adam could barely focus, let alone stand, and he began to stumble. He snapped out his hand and clamped it around one of the men's hands. Before any could realize what was happening, Adam fell backwards, pulling the man with him into the neon green abyss below. The fumes clouded Adam's mind even more, but the pain was perfectly clear when his body plunged into the terrible liquid.

"Eric!" one man called. He was short, but broad, his head resembling a cue ball. His brown eyes filled with hatred as he watched Adam and the other man, Eric, fall into the void below. "James, that freak just killed Eric!"

"Fucking monster!" the other man, James, replied, staring down at the fading images. He was tall, but very lanky, though his muscles had a strange tone. His black hair was in dread locks, and his skin was almost as dark, resembling the color of coffee beans. "You're gonna pay on behalf of your friend, bitch!"

Erin's fighting stance vanished and she fell to her knees. "Adam..." she whispered, hardly hearing the two killers storm towards her, "you can't leave me, too." She didn't resist at all when the two men grabbed her arms and lifted her into the air.

"Let's take her into that other room, Rob," James said. "These fumes will give me a damn headache if we do her here."

"Good call," the short man, Rob, replied.

It's all my fault, Erin thought. Once again, it's all my fault.

* * *

Hate.
Hate you.

50

I hate you all.

A dark figure stormed through the upper level of the complex, its clothing dripping with blood. It left a trail of bloody footsteps in its wake, leading back to mutilated corpses of two men. Now the figure followed the snowy tracks of the men's comrades.

I am the grim reaper.

I am your worst nightmare.

I hate you all.

* * *

Pain is all Adam could feel. His skin burned, melted and dissolved into nothing as he sank deeper into the abyss. Without evening realizing it, Adam's mind slowly cleared, his eyes rolled back into his skull and he began to speak to the only thing he know would listen.

God, please help me.

The pain Adam had felt up to this point was a paper cut in comparison to the anguish he felt he called out to God.

ABOMINATION! WHY DO YOU CALL TO ME?

Adam's eyes burned and his mind felt as if it was to split in two, yet he cried out to God again.

Father… please, help me.

FATHER? YOU ARE NO CHILD OF MINE!

I… I have to save Erin. Father…

Adam's body ceased to be in pain as a crawling sensation consumed his mind. Adam spoke firmly all of a sudden, almost as if making a demand.

Father. God. Yahweh. Allah. Give me the strength and will to save your follower, Erin. If I

51

cannot be your child, then let me save the one whom deserves to be called your daughter.

The pain returned, but somehow Adam knew it came with a blessing.

I RECOGNIZE YOU NOT, CREATURE, BUT THE LIGHT IS NOT FOREIGN TO YOUR HEART. GO, AND SAVE MY FOLLOWER, ERIN.

I will not fail, Father. I will not fail her.

Are you ready?

Yes.

Are you afraid?

Not anymore.

* * *

"Don't worry, baby," James cackled, "we're gonna treat you real good before we throw you in with your freaky friend."

"I call first dibs," Rob chimed in, "'cause you went first on that last broad."

"Fair enough. I like red heads too much to care about sloppy seconds anyway."

Adam, Erin thought, why did you have to leave me, too? Her body was frozen, lying frigid on the floor as the two men began to unzip her jumpsuit. This, she thought, is the end.

The two men stopped abruptly and turned towards the hole to see a withered hand clinging to the edge of the floor, followed by another hand. James grabbed Erin and held her as a human shield, aiming his gun at the hole. Rob stood on the other side of the room, also aiming his gun towards the hole. Both, however, lowered their hands from the shock of what they saw.

"No," Rob said, "there's no fucking way."

Pulling himself through the hole was Adam, though he hardly resembled the gentle man that had fallen into the sea of acid. Staring with a fiery hatred and simultaneous desperation, Adam stretched his withered arms forward, his hands grasping at the very air, as if there were something to grab on to. The fur coat had completely dissolved within the acid and his jumpsuit had begun to rip. His hair had mostly fallen out and his eyelids had melted away. His gums bled profusely, staining his teeth. He opened his mouth, coughing up blood, yet despite all the obviously agony that overwhelmed him, he took a step forward. The most shocking feature of all, however, was his wings. Not only were they unharmed, but they were now enormous. The joints came just past his shoulders, and from there the tips went to his ankles. Adam clenched his teeth and continued forward, acid still dripping from his body, skin sizzling and steaming as he stared ahead.

"What the hell is this guy?" James said in shock, almost losing his hold on Erin. "He just fell into a vat of acid!"

Adam groaned in pain with each step, slowly advancing towards the two men. "I won't…" Adam groaned, "…let you hurt her!"

"Oh, really?" Rob raised his gun back towards Adam and fired two bullets into Adam's right shoulder. "How about now? You sting enough, yet? I bet that acid really burns. It's what you deserve, freak!"

Erin watched in horror as Adam clenched his shoulder in so much pain he couldn't even scream. His eyes burned with anguish, rage, sorrow, confusion and madness, yet he looked back towards his assailants and continued to walk forward, each step a battle.

"Hot damn!" James snickered. "Look at him burn, man!" He smiled as the acid slowly ate away at Adam's flesh.

"Here's a little something to help you walk, freak!" Rob fired a bullet into Adam's left kneecap, sending the battered man to his knees, coughing up blood onto the floor.

"No!" Erin screamed. "Stop it!" Her eyes filled with tears and soaked her cheeks. "Adam…"

Adam's own eyes began to stream tears down his face, but he couldn't stop. He clenched his teeth so tight that his already bleeding gums produced a waterfall, pouring blood onto his jumpsuit as he pushed himself off the ground.

"Rob," James sighed, "just fucking kill him. I'm getting a little anxious over here, man."

Rob laughed. "Yeah, I guess you're right." He aimed the gun at Adam's head. "It's been fun, freak, but it's time to die." He grinned wickedly. "Any last w-"

Rob's voice was suddenly cut off, along with his head. Blood splashed across the floor and his head rolled towards Adam's feet. Dripping with Rob's blood was a cruelly curved scythe, and it continued to hack away at the headless corpse until it was nothing but a pile of bloody chunks of flesh and bone. The scythe slowly rose into the air and hovered, awaiting its master's command. James swung his arm away from Adam and pointed it towards the newcomer. "What the…" he stammered. "Who the fuck are you?"

"Kyle…" Adam whispered, almost choking on his own blood.

Kyle's face couldn't have appeared angrier, nor could it have appeared more hurt. His clothes and face dripped with blood and his eyes brimmed with hatred and sorrow. "My baby sister," Kyle hissed. "You killed my baby sister!" Kyle clenched his teeth and the sorrow in his eyes was buried by his anger. "I hate you! I hate you all!" He turned to Adam. "And I especially hate you, doll! If it wasn't for you..." Kyle's rage burned in Adam's mind, almost as much as the acid burned his flesh. "If Nathan had never found you, he would've never returned to this place... he would've never left Layla alone to die!" Kyle's own gums began to bleed, his teeth clenched so tight it was a wonder they didn't crack. "It's your fault my baby sister's dead! You killed Layla!"

Kyle immediately toppled over, screaming in pain and clutching his right leg as blood poured from the bullet holes.

"Oh, shut the fuck up!" James shouted, smoke coming from his gun. "Crying like a little bitch isn't going to bring your precious whore of a sister back! Be a man and suck it up!" He aimed his gun at Kyle's head. "Don't you want to die with some dignity?"

What are you doing?
It hurts to move.
You have to stop James.
I can't.
You have to save your friends.
It hurts.
...Kyle was right.
What?
You are just a doll, aren't you?
No.
A useless...

Stop it.

...worthless...

Shut up.

...doll.

"No!" Adam screamed, his body propelling forward towards James. He shot his hand forward, reaching for James' face. James had no time to react before Adam's hand was clasped tight around his face and forced him to the ground, causing James to lose his grip on Erin, as well as his gun. "I will... break you!"

Erin stumbled to the side, smacking against the wall. "My God..." she whispered in amazement.

"Adam?" Kyle said, as if waking up from a trance. "You... why did you...?"

"You will never... hurt another person... again!" Adam screamed with rage down into James' face as his hand slowly began to crush James' cheek bones. Adam felt the bones cracking, his mind surging with James's fear and anger. Slowly, the sound of cracking bone grew louder and finally James' cheek bones crushed inward. James' eyes went wide with pain, and Adam felt James' hot breath on his hand. The pain was too overwhelming to allow James to scream.

"Die, you monster!" Adam screamed, raising his hand into air, balling it into a fist. "Die!" Adam began to smash his fist against James' chest, each hit making a louder cracking noise, as James' rib cage slowly gave way to the beating. Adam then spread his hand across James' chest and dug his nails into James' skin. Adam's fingers pierced James' flesh and clenched his ruined ribcage, and, drawing upon all his might, anger, sorrow, confusion and fear, Adam ripped the ribcage in two.

Dropping the shards of bone to the ground, Adam once again balled his hand into a fist.

"Go to Hell," Adam screamed, "where you belong!" Adam's fist plummeted downward and, with no ribs to act as a shield, smashed James' heart, spraying blood into Adam's face.

Erin shook with horror, her stomach turning. "Adam… what… happened to you?"

Kyle slowly stoop up, using his scythe as a crutch. "I'll… be damned."

You did it.

Yes, I did.

Are you all right?

Yes, I am.

Do you know now what you are?

I am what I perceive myself to be.

And what is that?

Wings of an angel, blood of a demon: I am indeed an abomination, but I do not perceive myself to be one.

What then?

A friend.

Part III: Toy Soldier

Chapter IX

Wake up.

Who's there?

I'm your better half.

Who the fuck are you?

Wake up, Kyle.

Kyle snapped awake and sat up in cold sweat. What the hell kind of dream was that, Kyle thought. Kyle looked around the room and took a minute to get his bearings. He was still uneasy about living in the science facility, but Nathan insisted it was for the best. Adam, he said, was too weak to travel anyway.

"Adam..." Kyle whispered, "you... bastard." Kyle smashed his fist against the steel floor. "Layla dies because of you...and Nathan treats you like some kind of hero." Kyle closed his eyes. "Fucking... doll."

* * *

"Are you feeling any better, Adam?" Erin asked.

Adam looked up from the floor, gingerly rubbing his eyes, and smiled at Erin. His eyelids had regenerated, and his skin was as smooth as it had ever been, except for several faint scars from bullet holes. His hair, however, was still very short, barely half an inch. The locks of hair that remained from when he had climbed out of the acid a week ago had to be cut, and now Adam could only wait for his hair to grow back. "Yes," he said, "I do. My eyes burn occasionally, and my scalp tends to itch every so often, but I feel better."

Erin smiled, relieved that Adam was no longer in serious pain. "I'm sure those little discomforts will go away soon." Erin tilted her head slightly. "But if it really starts to bother you, we could inject some-"

"No," Adam said firmly, bringing his hands to his head, his fingers tracing across his stubbles of hair. "I told you, it makes my blood boil just looking at that... slime."

"But it's really helped Nathan and Kyle! You can't even tell they were shot! Maybe if we injected just a little-"

"No. Absolutely not."

Erin nodded, sighing softly. "All right, sorry I brought it up."

Adam had meant to refer to the serum as poison, because just thinking of it made him sick to his stomach. After Adam had killed the James, the group searched frantically for some form of medical supplies. On the opposite end of the corridor from the acid room, there was what appeared to be an infirmary. There was an abundance of medicine, bandages and a litany of other supplies, but what the group took the greatest notice of were two racks of a dozen syringes full of a blood-red liquid. Below the rack was a label that read "Experimental Regenerative Serum." With Nathan on his death bed and Kyle growing delirious from blood loss, Erin and Adam took each took a syringe and injected the contents into their wounded companions without bothering to question the origins of the vial, or the strange convenience. Adam, however, was convinced that they probably should have. The second he touched the syringe, Adam felt his blood boil and his skin crawl. The others felt nothing of the sort, however, and insisted that Adam was still suffering from the shock of the acid. But Adam knew the difference. Adam knew that something was very wrong with those serums, and he would die before he took a single drop into his body.

"I'm not interrupting anything, am I?" Nathan called from the doorway, a grin spread across this face.

"Nathan, you've been a bit of a dickhead lately," Erin said flatly. "No, Adam and I were just talking about how he's feeling."

"You two talk an awful lot."

"Adam is much easier to talk to than a borderline psychotic or a technology geek." Erin looked at Adam and winked playfully. "And he's so much cuter."

Adam felt his cheeks heat up and he glanced towards Nathan, then Erin, then back to Nathan. "Kyle's only border line?"

Nathan and Erin burst out laughing. The real humor laid in the fact that Adam had intended it as a legitimate question, not a joke. "Adam," Nathan said, trying to calm himself down, "you're great, man! Absolutely great!"

Adam darted his eyes back and forth between Erin and Nathan, his face still hot. "Thank you."

"Is Kyle still sleeping?" Erin asked.

* * *

Am I dreaming?

If you mean dreaming as in envisioning a collage of meaningless, subconscious thoughts, then no. If you mean dreaming as in being exposed to a wealth of opportunity, then yes.

What the hell are you talking about?

Have you ever wondered what it's like to be a god?

Well, yeah, but… wait, what does that have to do with anything?

You can make your dreams reality. I can show you the way.

Who are you?

I am you.

What the fuck does that mean?

I am your desire to tower over the weak. I am your need to grow in power. I am your obsession with destruction.

Destruction?

Adam.

The doll? What about him?

We wish to see him fall. We wish to see him suffer. We wish to see him dead.

Why?

Adam is stronger than you. You are an insect compared to him. You are at his mercy.

No fucking way in hell! I'm superior in every way imaginable to that doll!

It angers you. It hurts you. It drives you mad. I can show you how we can destroy him.

You? Me? We? You're not making any sense!

You are the vessel, but it is weak without conviction. I am conviction, but it is useless without a vessel. But together, we are a god amongst insects.

Where did you come from?

Do you believe in God?

"Kyle?"

Kyle snapped out of his daze and looked up to see Erin and Nathan standing in the doorway of the infirmary. "You all right, man?" Nathan asked.

"I'm fucking fine," Kyle replied. "What is it?"

"We were going to search the archives for some information on this place. We figured you might want to join us, in case we come across anything interesting."

"Where's Adam?"

"He's already there, waiting for us. You coming or you just want to sleep?"

Kyle clenched his teeth, but sealed his lips to not let on. Adam is not superior, he thought, he's just a fucking doll. He stood up and nodded. "Lead the way, you two."

* * *

Adam shifted uncomfortably in his new outfit as he sat on the floor in front of the glowing pillar. The lockers in the infirmary also had what must have been personnel uniforms. The outfit looked more like riot armor, however, and was terribly hard to move in. Not only that, but the holes made for his wings took forever to make, were to small and squeezed the base of his wings like a boa constrictor. Nathan had thought it made him look "hard as hell." Kyle had told him it made him look like a toy soldier instead of just a doll. Erin had smacked Kyle in the back of the head.

You've been recovering nicely.

Adam blinked and raised his head a little. It had been a week since the voice had said anything.

Nice of you to fit me into your schedule.

How human you've become.

What are you talking about?

A week ago, you would have not responded in such a manner.

I guess not.

I have a question for you.

Normally, I'm the one with all the questions.

You and I aren't normal.

What's your question?

What do you perceive yourself to be?

I told you: a friend.

A friend is something a person is to other people. You act as a friend, but a friend isn't a state of being.

What are you saying?

I'm saying I need you to look at yourself and tell me what you perceive yourself to be.

I answered y-

Your answer is unsatisfactory.

Don't try to pull that on me! I've gotten nothing but unsatisfactory answers from you since day one, but you never clarify one bit!

What do you perceive yourself to be?

I'm done talking to you.

What do you perceive yourself to be?

Leave me alone!

What do you perceive yourself to be?

Shut up!

What do you perceive yourself to be?

"Nothing!" Adam screamed. "I perceive myself as nothing! Leave me alone! Leave me alone! I hate you! I hate you!"

"Adam?"

Adam leapt to his feet and spun around to see Kyle, Nathan and Erin standing there, spellbound. His face grew hot and his hands began to tremble as his eyes darted back and forth from each of the three.

"Adam," Erin said softly as she took a step forward, "what's wrong?"

Adam looked down at the floor. Then, the floor began to move beneath him. He saw the feet of his companions flash past his eyes as the floor continued to sweep him away faster and faster. Behind him he heard his companions' voices calling out to him, but they faded more and more.

64

Suddenly, the floor was no more and he was looking up the elevator shaft and his body propelled upward. The broken gears and frayed wires whizzed past him in a great blur until he was out of the shaft and flying over the floor on the first floor of the complex. Brilliant white light engulfed his body, and Adam watched as the metal floor transformed into mounds of snow which grew smaller and smaller until finally darkness clouded his vision, and Adam retreated from the cold reality that surrounded him.

Chapter X

Adam slowly opened his eyes and found himself lying in a small mound of snow. As Adam began to push himself up, his body trembled in pain and he collapsed back into the snow. Adam's legs burned as if they had been dipped back into the vat of acid, and his wings ached as if they had been crushed under the heel of a giant. How did I get here, he thought as he turned his head from side to side. Adam once again tried to push himself up off the ground, but could only drag his body along the ground; his legs refused to move and his wings had become like lead. Slowly, Adam crawled from the mound of snow towards what seemed to be a small wall. Adam clawed at the wall and pulled himself up. He leaned his body against the wall and rested his belly upon it. It was then that Adam realized he wasn't leaning on a wall, but a ledge that over looked the frozen ruins of a city. Down below, moving like a chaotic horde of ants, countless people scurried about through the snow from building to building, stopping every so often to talk to one another.

"Where…" Adam whispered to himself. "Where am I?"

* * *

"Where the hell could he have gone?" Nathan bellowed, half concerned and half annoyed. "What the hell got into him?"

"Maybe the acid fucked with his head more than we thought," Kyle suggested, actually trying to be somewhat helpful.

"Kyle! You're not helping!" Erin shouted.

"Oh fuck you!" Kyle snapped back. "The one time in history that I decide to be somewhat concerned and all you can do-"

"Shut up!" Nathan yelled. "Shut the hell up, both of you! We have to find him and we have to start looking now!"

"Where the hell are we going to look?" Kyle said, throwing his arms into the air. "He's got fucking wings! He could be anywhere!"

"Well, we'll just have to look anywhere!" Nathan walked over to the shelf where he had put their cache of weaponry that they had taken from the raiders. "Take what you can carry, lock and load and let's get moving."

"What?" Kyle scratched his head. "Nathan, I've got my own-"

"Your antiques be damned! There are way too many strange fucking things going on and I'm not about to have your outdated weapons guarding my back." Nathan picked up Layla's old shotgun and threw it to Kyle, who caught it with a look of reverence. "Why are there so many raiders in this area all of a sudden? This region has been practically uninhabited for years except for us, and now it's suddenly crawling with raiders!" He picked up an assault rifle and examined it and held it up for the others to see. "What's stranger is their gear! They were packing weapons that we haven't even found in military bases and they were in top condition! Look at this rifle: no rust, no dents, not even any fucking scratches!" He threw the rifle to Erin who caught it, but just barely, almost as if she was afraid to hold it. "Something's going on that shouldn't be, and I'm not going to rely on a scythe, machete and pair of fists. If you've got so serious a problem that you can't use these weapons, then don't fucking bother helping me find Adam, because you're nothing more than dead weight." He picked up a submachine gun and turned off the safety. "Are you with me?"

* * *

Adam eased himself down behind the ledge and rubbed his sore legs, trying to think how he got there. I saw the floor, he thought, the walls and the ceiling rush past me. I saw the snow and sky and light and then nothing. Maybe I ran and then flew away, but I don't remember running. It just happened. That would explain why I blacked out, I suppose, and why my wings and legs are so tired.

Adam scratched his head and closed his eyes. His legs and wings began to tingle and he felt his muscles slowly relaxing. Can't do anything until my legs stop aching, Adam thought, might as well just rest for a little while.

* * *

"I'm not going," Kyle said firmly.

"What do you mean you're not going?" Erin shrieked, throwing her arms into the air.

"I mean I'm not going." Kyle walked over to the pile of weapons and reverently set Layla's shotgun down next to her katanas. "I'm staying here."

"You son of a bitch," Nathan shouted, "how can you just stay here when Adam's lost out there?"

"How?" Kyle turned and looked Nathan straight in the eyes. "How can I stay here?" His hands balled into fists and he began to scream right in Nathan's face. "I'll tell you how I can fucking stay here, asshole! Layla's dead because of him! If we hadn't found his sorry ass, you wouldn't have bothered coming back here looking for your fucking treasure!" Kyle grabbed Nathan by the collar of his coat and brought his face a bare inch from Kyle's. "Let your goddamn doll freeze to death or get shot by raiders or fucking walk off a cliff! I don't care!" Kyle pushed Nathan back and took a few steps backward himself. "I don't care if you die looking for him, either." Kyle glanced over at Erin and then back at Nathan, and then he turned and walked out of the room.

"Nathan," Erin said softly, "what are we going to do?"

"Fuck, fine!" Nathan shouted after Kyle, ignoring Erin completely. "Go on and pout, Kyle! Go right ahead! We'll find Adam without your sorry ass!" He turned towards Erin. "C'mon, Erin, let's go." He immediately headed for the door, and Erin slowly turned and followed.

Adam, she thought, please don't leave me. Don't leave me like mama.

Chapter XI

Soaring across the sky, a steel construct descended from the clouds towards the frozen wastes below. Glowing, circular pads covered the bottom, the brilliant light diminishing as the construct propelled towards the ground. Faster and faster it descended and then abruptly stopped, touching down upon the icy remains of a city block. A hole formed on the side of construct, and four men in steel suits marched out into the snow, each armed with the finest heavy weaponry seen in ages. The men created a perimeter around the construct and waited in silence. A fifth figure emerged from the hole of the construct and walked out into the snow. The figure, a stunningly attractive man, surveyed the surroundings and brought his left index finger to his temple. He was tall and well built, his muscles rippling through his blue and white jumpsuit, and his blonde, crew-cut hair gave clear indication to service in some form of military. His finger touched upon a small block of metal which glowed a pale blue. His right eye gave forth a faint, golden glow, one that would have drawn attention to the long scar over his eye socket had anyone been there to see him. His hand dropped to his side and he looked ahead.

"The mercenaries have failed," the man said. His voice commanded the attention of the men of steel and they all turned to look at him. "I shall locate the Harbinger and deal with it myself. You will stay and guard the ship. Kill all that approach."

A sudden wind began to swirl around the man and he leapt into the air and landed on top of a nearby building. He surveyed the surrounding area and again leapt into the air and began to rapidly stride from roof top to roof top.

"You cannot hide from me," the man said. "I will find you." He leapt across two buildings and landed on the tallest building within sight. "I will obliterate you."

* * *

I can show you how to destroy Adam.

I know how to kill. I've done it plenty of times.

You've never killed one such as Adam.

I will in time.

Only if you swallow that foolish pride and let me guide you.

I don't need you or anyone else. That doll is n-

You pale to him!

Kyle's face hardened and his eyes burned with hatred. He clenched his teeth so hard his bottom-left molar cracked. Within Kyle's icy blue eyes, a yellow spark glimmered like an ember.

If you wish to kill Adam, you must obey me unquestioningly.

Am I going insane, Kyle thought. Why am I hearing this voice? Why am I so obsessed with Adam?

Are you ready to listen?

Yes.

Physically and mentally, you are nothing to Adam.

I thought you were going to help me.

Emotionally, however, Adam is a mere child. It is there you shall find a way to conquer him.

What are you talking about?

You have to keep what he loves safe until you are in position to destroy it.

What he loves? You mean…

Yes.

No… no, you can't mean that.

Yes.

I can't just…

You must kill Erin.

Cold sweat trickled down Kyle's face. He wasn't best of friends with Erin. He never was, really, nor was he a great friend of Nathan's, but they were still friends of a sort. What would Layla think, Kyle thought, if I killed Erin? No, Adam killed Layla. It's his fault. But... how can I?

You must kill Erin when Adam can do nothing but watch.

* * *

Adam stood up after a rather non-refreshing nap in an incredibly uncomfortable position and stretched out his arms, legs and wings. After a minute or so, Adam gently flapped his wings, enough to make a soft gust but not lift him off the ground. It then occurred to him that he never actually consciously attempted to fly.

Adam walked over to the edge of the building and stepped onto the ledge and stretched his wings. Okay, Adam thought, I did this before. Not exactly on purpose, but I still did it. Let's see what I can do!

Adam stretched his wings and raised them as high above his head as he could and flapped them downward as hard as he could. Immediately, Adam was flung into the air, caught completely off guard. It was simply amazing. At least, it was until gravity kicked in and he started to fall. Adam began to panic and flapped his wings frantically in short spurts of uneven strength. Adam's side smashed against the ledge and he spun uncontrollably downward along the side of the building into an icy alleyway, right on top of some trash cans.

Adam yelped in pain as he laid crumpled in a ball on top of the crushed trash cans. Slowly, Adam climbed to his feet and shook the snow off of his body. Adam cleared his mind and took a deep breath. Okay, Adam thought, just think about what you need to do. Adam bent at the knees and raised his wings as high as he could and again flapped his wings down as hard as he could. Adam propelled upward, but this time Adam raised his wings as his body shot up. As his body began to slow, Adam's wings flapped back down, propelling him further into the air. He continued until he was clear of the building and high into the air, the people below mere specks. He raised his wings one more time but flapped with only half the strength from before, resulting in a very minor upward motion. He continued to flap his wings, realizing he could hover at a given altitude with the current pressure. He leaned his body forward and his wings carried him gently through air.

"Well," Adam said, "how about that?" He smiled softly and gazed down at the frozen landscape. Despite the destruction and obvious chaos that lay beneath him, it was beautiful from up high and, somehow, familiar. Adam looked forward to the sky and nodded to the clouds. Adam raised his wings and flapped them as hard as he could and propelled himself forward, occasionally holding his wings straight and gliding through the air. "Better get back before everyone starts worrying."

* * *

"Nathan," Erin said as he nervously fingered the assault rifle, "I'm worried about Adam."

"I know," Nathan replied, "I'm worried too." Nathan twirled the submachine gun around his finger like a cowboy as he looked back at Erin. "We have to keep moving, though, otherwise some raiders might find him first."

Erin lowered her head in silence. He looked at the rifle and then back at Nathan. "What if he's hurt? What if-"

Nathan put a finger to her lips. "Erin, I didn't mean to get you more worried than you already are. Adam is one tough son of a bitch, and no one on earth is a match for him. I just meant that it'd be best if we found him so he doesn't get hurt too bad." He smiled faintly. "C'mon, he can dodge bullets, smash bones and fly, for Christ's sake! He'll be fine."

Erin smiled softly and nodded. "Yeah, you're right. Adam can take care of himself." She laughed softly and shook her head. "C'mon, let's find Adam."

"That's the spirit! We'll find him in no time if we keep that attitude!" Nathan held the submachine gun in the air, triumphantly, like they had already found him. "Onward!"

Erin laughed and held the rifle in the air along with Nathan's gun. "Onward!"

Just then, the two heard footsteps in the distance. They turned towards to sound and saw a figure in black running towards them. They began to raise their weapons, but lowered them when they saw a scythe strapped to the figure's back and a shotgun in its hands.

"Well," Nathan said, putting one hand on his hip, "look who decided to join us."

"Didn't want you two ladies to get yourselves killed," Kyle said as he approached Nathan and Erin.

"And just what are you implying, Kyle?" Erin said sharply.

"That Nathan is a woman and women are inferior to men, of course."

"Keep talking, Kyle, and you'll be wearing your balls as a bow tie, and we'll see how damn superior you are."

"I do cherish these moments," Nathan said with a smile.

"That is good," a dark voice called from the distance, "for it shall be the last moment of your lives."

The three spun around, weapons drawn and ready, and faced the source of the voice. About ten meters away stood a tall, comely man in a blue and white jumpsuit. In his right hand was a black, oversized revolver, with a barrel so wide a quarter could probably get lodged inside of it. A golden light flickered in his right eye, drawing attention to a long scar across his eye socket.

"The allies of the Harbinger," he said, his voice like a dagger of ice, "must perish."

Chapter XII

"Harbinger?" Nathan said, confused. "Allies? What the hell?"

"Hey," Kyle whispered, "isn't that the same jumpsuit Adam had on when we found him?"

"Hey, you're right," Erin whispered back, "it is!" What... what do you think that means?"

The man raised his arm and pointed the revolver towards the three. "Today," he said "you shall fall to the might of Ahadiel." A golden light flickered in his right eye.

"Ahadiel?" Kyle repeated. "What the f-"

A giant flare burst forth from the barrel of the man's gun and a terrible sound echoed throughout the snow covered street. Debris exploded forth from a pillar of a nearby building that towered behind the three. The man, Ahadiel, pulled back the hammer on his revolver and took a wide step to his right.

"Holy shit!" Kyle screamed and he pulled the trigger on Layla's shotgun. The window of a ruined car behind Ahadiel shattered and the shards flew in a thousand different directions.

"Oh hell!" Nathan gritted his teeth and pulled the trigger on the submachine gun while reaching for his pistol with his free hand. Bullets flew across the street in a wild spray, pinging against the ruined car and the building behind it.

"My god..." Erin stood frozen, the weapon in her hand suddenly seeming like a lead weight. Her fingers went cold and everything seemed to slow down and the volume of her surroundings faded.

Ahadiel tilted his head ever-so slightly to the right and pulled the trigger of his revolver. Again, a great flare and a horrible sound burst forth from the barrel of the gun. Blood splashed over Kyle's left arm and Erin's right side as Kyle's hand exploded, his fingers spinning away into the air as his body spun to the left and fell backwards. Ahadiel took another step to the right, his left leg crossing over his right, and he pulled back the hammer once more.

"Fuck!" Kyle screamed, the stump on his left hand pouring out blood. His right hand dropped the shotgun as he collapsed hard on to the ground and he reached for his pistol. His mind was a blur and his vision no better as pain surged throughout his arm and upper back.

"Shit, shit, shit, shit!" Nathan held down the trigger on the submachine gun as he extended his other arm which held his pistol. He pulled the trigger on his pistol and sent forth an extra bullet to once again miss Ahadiel and add further damage to the car behind him.

Erin couldn't speak. She could hardly breathe. Ahadiel dodged each bullet like it was part of a dance. Each step was graceful. Every motion of his body was fluid. She no longer heard the explosions of the guns or the screaming of her friends. All she could think about was her dead mother, blood pouring from a lone bullet hole in her neck.

Ahadiel bent at the hips, as if he were bowing. His arm remained extended as his body spun in a circle, his weight still shifting towards the right as he balanced upon his left foot. With only 90 degrees left to complete the circle, Ahadiel pulled the trigger. The flare and noise was followed by a great splash of blood across Nathan's left leg from the newly added gaping hole. The strong man collapsed to his side, spinning slightly. Ahadiel completed the circle and set his right foot back onto the ground and again he pulled back the hammer.

"You son of a bitch!" Kyle extended his right arm and pulled the trigger on his pistol. The ball bullet sped towards Ahadiel's foot and did nothing but spray snow upon the assailant's leg. Sweat poured down Kyle's face and clouded his eyes, mixing with his tears from the agony that flowed through his body.

"Mother fucker!" The submachine gun ran out of ammo as Nathan's left side crashed to the ground. He dropped it and continued to pull the trigger on his pistol, either blasting holes into the side of the now obliterated car or shooting up snow onto Ahadiel's legs. His vision clouded and suddenly his mind flashed the image of lying on the ground in the science facility, bleeding and waiting to die.

Mama, Erin thought, I can't do this. I can't shoot him. I can't hurt someone the way you were hurt. I can't kill. I can't kill. I can't kill. Mama, please, help me. Please.

Ahadiel suddenly shifted his weigh to his left. His left leg took a wide step to the left and he pulled the trigger. Giant shards of debris exploded from the building behind the three and rolled across the ground. His right leg crossed over his left and he pulled the hammer back.

"Fuck, Erin, shoot him!" Kyle was now completely helpless. He was too weak and disabled to use the shotgun and had no hope of reloading his pistol in any timely manner.

"Erin, what the fuck are you waiting for?" The snow ran red with Nathan's blood and sweat coated his face as his pistol clicked. There was no more ammo left. He reached into his coat and fumbled for an extra clip as his body trembled with a mix of cold and fear.

No, Erin thought, I can't. I won't. I won't hurt anyone that way. I don't want to see anyone in that kind of pain. Mama, I won't do it. I won't. I won't hurt anyone like I hurt you.

Ahadiel's left leg swung out from behind his right and he pulled the trigger once more. Erin toppled backwards as blood burst out of her shoulder, her bones shattering like glass. Ahadiel stood firm in his position as he watched her collapse to the ground. He pulled back the hammer, loading the final bullet into the chamber.

"Erin!" Kyle looked at Erin and watched her shake like a little girl who had been hit by her father. I'm dead, he thought.

"Erin!" Nathan dropped the fresh clip of ammo into the snow as he watched Erin screaming on the ground. This is the end, he thought.

Erin's senses heightened to peaks she had only experienced once in her life. Everything was still. Silent. Frozen. Kyle and Nathan were still-life images. All that moved was Ahadiel. All that made noise was Ahadiel. All that mattered was Ahadiel. Erin screamed and pulled the trigger on the rifle.

Ahadiel's body twisted and rolled in sporadic jerks and directions, narrowly avoiding each bullet. Then, probability caught up with him. A bullet grazed across his left cheek and jerked his head slightly to the side, leaving a long, red cut. The bullets stopped coming at him and he steadied himself. He aimed the revolver at Erin's chest and pulled the trigger.

A flare.

A noise.

A miracle.

"No... fucking way." Kyle looked at Erin and then looked upward in disbelief.

"I don't... believe it." Nathan stared upward, no longer feeling the pain in his leg, and the pistol slipped out of his hand.

Mama, Erin thought, you sent help. Mama... thank you.

A black mass towered in front of Erin. On the ground beneath it, laid the bullet that was intended to end Erin's life, steaming in the snow. The mass held perfectly still for what seemed to be an eternity. Then the front of the mass opened up and a hardened face appeared from within.

"Game over," Adam said firmly, his eyes locked onto to Ahadiel as his wings folded behind his back.

Ahadiel's face lit up, as did his right eye. The golden glow faded and Ahadiel dropped his gun. "I've found you, at last, Harbinger."

Adam turned and looked behind him. "Get out of here. Now. I'll take care of him."

"Harbinger?" Nathan said, coughing. "Did he just-"

"I said 'get out of here!'"

That did the trick. The three forced themselves to their feet and Erin and Kyle each gave Nathan a shoulder to lean on and the three scurried away. Adam looked back at Ahadiel and glared at him with great hatred burning in his eyes.

"I've been waiting for this day, Harbinger," Ahadiel said. "Today, I will realize what I'm truly capable of."

"Today," Adam said coldly, "will be the last day of your life."

80

Chapter XIII

Blood ran down the side of Ahadiel's face, staining his jumpsuit. As Adam and Ahadiel stared each other down, the cut across Ahadiel's cheek sealed. The golden light flickered in Ahadiel's right eye and the block of metal on the side of his head emitted a pale blue glow. A grin stretched across his face, and he began to walk towards Adam.

"You're awfully happy," Adam said gravely, "for a dead man."

"I've always wondered what it would be like to meet the legendary Angelic Harbinger," Ahadiel said, slowly moving closer and closer toward Adam. "You're not exactly what I expected." His eye flickered and his grin widened. "But you're enough for me."

Adam clenched his fists and hardened his expression as Ahadiel crept closer and closer and closer. "I don't know what you're talking about, nor do I care." His eyes locked with Ahadiel's. "You hurt my friends. You hurt Erin. You will never hurt another again."

Ahadiel stopped a few meters before Adam. "Your wings will be my trophy, Harbinger." He raised his hands and held them out, his shoulders relaxed, as if he were welcoming Adam. "Are you ready?"

* * *

"Who the fuck was that?" Kyle screamed, blood still gushing from his hand.

"How the fuck should I know?" Nathan screamed back, holding on to both Kyle and Erin as he limped through the snow, blood cascading down his leg onto the snow.

"Well, he sure as hell knew us!" Erin screamed as she tried her best to help support Nathan, despite her ruined shoulder.

The three trudged through the snow towards the science facility, their blood creating a plainly visible trail behind them. Once inside and at the elevator shaft, the three were faced with a rather embarrassing difficulty. Kyle, however, was more concerned with something else.

Why am I still alive, Kyle thought. He shot my hand off, I'm bleeding non-stop. I should be dead. He turned his head towards Erin, and the pain suddenly numbed significantly. You worthless bitch, he thought. Why didn't you shoot him right away? I lost my fucking hand because of you.

Kyle stepped away from Nathan, letting him topple to the ground, pulling Erin with him. He reached behind his back and pulled his scythe from its straps and stormed over to the elevator. I can take care of myself, he thought, forget them.

"Kyle!" Nathan shouted. "What the fuck are you doing?"

"You prick!" Erin screamed. "Get back here!"

Kyle didn't respond. He looked down the shaft and leapt forward. He drove his scythe into the wall and turned his head away, sparks flew as he slid down the wall, watching the door flash past his eyes. As the door to the floor of the infirmary came into view, he slammed his feet against the wall and kicked himself, along with his scythe, off the wall and through the door. He barrel rolled down the hallway, cutting his face on his own scythe, but had made it all the same, and he stormed off down the hallway towards the infirmary.

They'll die.

I don't care.

Erin has to live long enough for-
I don't care.

Don't you want to avenge Layla?
Kyle stopped dead in his tracks. What did you say, he thought.

Your sister deserves vengeance. Are you just going to let Adam get away with your sister's death?
No... I won't. You're right, Layla deserves vengeance! But how? You said I wasn't strong enough.

If you do as I tell you, you will be a god. And no one, not even Adam, can oppose you.
Where did you come from?

Hell.
How did you get into my head?

I'm in your very blood, Kyle. The serum you injected into yourself was my blood.
You're... a demon?

Yes. I am the greatest of all demons.
Then how did some scientists get their hands on your blood? Must not have been that great.

Enough of your questions. Now you will listen.
Fine, I'm listening.

Go to the infirmary and inject yourself with all but three vials of the serum. Smash all the used vials, as well as one unused one and say that you knocked it over. Bring the remaining two with you to Erin and Nathan. Inject a vial in each of them. Do you understand?
Yes.

Power will be ours soon, Kyle. We will be like God.

Kyle picked himself up off the floor, delirious, blood still flowing from his hand. His body was covered in cold sweat as he stumbled towards the infirmary. Like God, Kyle thought. I never believed in God, but I think I like the sound of it anyway.

* * *

Adam felt the wind whip at his face, the cold air seemingly stirred by Ahadiel's challenge. Adam stood firm for several seconds and then lunged forward, rolling his body slightly to the right. His right wing swung around his body and the joint was pointed forward, like an elbow of a giant arm, while his left wing pointed straight back. Ahadiel brought up his left arm just in time for Adam's wing to smash against the back of Ahadiel's lower arm. His right foot shot back and slammed against the ground, bracing himself as Adam's weight pushed against him. He shot his right arm forward at Adam's chest. Adam's left hand clasped around Ahadiel's fist and Adam spun to his left, his right wing sliding off Ahadiel's arm and Adam's left wing swinging forward and smashing Ahadiel in the right temple, sending him hurdling through the air and crashing to the ground upon his left arm.

Got you, Adam thought. Adam ran towards Ahadiel as he laid upon the ground. Adam swung his right arm backwards and shot it down at Ahadiel's neck. Ahadiel rolled onto his right side and pushed his body off the ground with his elbow, Adam's fist whizzing harmlessly past Ahadiel's nose, and he clasped his left hand behind Adam's head and smashed his face against the ground. Adam's right canine pierced his lip and blood splashed out onto the snow as Ahadiel grinded his face against the frozen street. Ahadiel snapped out his hands and each grabbed one of Adam's wings. Ahadiel spun in circles and hurled Adam against the ruined car nearby, the windows shattering as the side of the car crushed beneath Adam's body, the glass slicing the back of Adam's uniform.

Got you, Ahadiel thought. He held out his right hand like a dagger and thrust it forward at Adam's chest. Adam's hands shot out and clasped around Ahadiel's wrist, stopping him dead in his tracks. Adam wrapped his legs around Ahadiel's waist and then Adam began to flap his wings and lift the two into the air. Twenty meters in the air, he stopped abruptly and the two plummeted to the ground, and Ahadiel's back crashed against the icy street, the impact shattering the ice that blanketed the street in a meter radius around the two men. Adam's left hand slid down to Ahadiel's elbow and hammered his fist against the back of it, breaking the joint and causing Ahadiel a world of pain.

Ahadiel snapped his left hand around Adam's neck and squeezed with all his might, enough for Adam's legs to release Ahadiel's waist. He pushed off the ground and leapt into the air, pulling Adam along by his throat. Thirty meters in the air, gravity took control and dragged the two back to the ground. Ahadiel positioned Adam beneath him and sent Adam's back crashing down upon the broken shards of ice below. Again, the impact was incredible, shattering even more of the icy blanket surrounding them. Adam cried out in pain as the shards dug into his back, blood seeping out onto the street.

Adam threw his legs up and rolled the two backwards, positioning him back on top of Ahadiel. With Ahadiel still holding Adam's neck in a death grip, Adam began to smash his fists against

Ahadiel's jaw over and over again. Ahadiel's molars dug into his cheeks and finally pierced through, creating gaping holes. Blood poured from Ahadiel's cheeks as the beating continued.

Ahadiel sent his left knee into Adam's stomach, creating a minor pause in the beating. Ahadiel quickly thrust his right knee into Adam's stomach as well, followed by another bash from the left. Ahadiel sat up ever so slightly and brought Adam's face within a hair's width oh his and began to smash his forehead into Adam's nose. Blood gushed forth from Adam's nostrils onto Ahadiel's face.

The pain surged throughout Adam's body: his back, his lip, his nose, his neck. His left eye snapped shut, not having the energy to keep both open. Through his squinted right eye, he saw Ahadiel's right eye flicker with that golden light, almost mocking him. Adam balled his left hand into a fist and slammed it against Ahadiel's right eye again and again. Finally, Ahadiel released Adam's neck and punched him in the forehead. Adam flew backwards off of Ahadiel, whose left hand clamped over his right eye. Adam sat up, his arms shaking as they held up his own weight, and watched as blood poured out from beneath Ahadiel's hand. Then, sparks shot from between Ahadiel's fingers and were followed by his own blood curdling screams.

The two men lied on the ground, groaning in agony. Then, there was silence as the wind picked up, blowing snow over the two broken combatants. The clouds rolled over the ruined city and fresh snow began to rapidly descend upon the streets, blanketing everything within several miles of the two men. As the storm raged on, Ahadiel began to laugh. With each cackle he coughed in pain. Adam slowly lifted his back off the ground, his arms still shaking, and looked at Ahadiel.

"Incredible," Ahadiel coughed. "Simply... incredible. Despite your heritage, despite my training... despite our shared blood... we are equal." Ahadiel laughed even harder, his coughing persisting. He dropped his bloody left hand away from his eye and to the ground, revealing his ruined right eye, a disturbing mix of blood, flesh, glass and circuitry.

Adam's arms finally failed and his bloody back smashed against the glass-like shards of ice, adding to his pain. Ahadiel, he thought, what are you? My heritage? Our blood? What am I? What are we?

The snow continued to bury the city, and slowly covered the two men. Adam's sight turned white and then all was black. I'm right where I started, Adam thought. Alone in the dark, freezing.

Part IV: Gateway to the Sky

Chapter XIV

Adam, are you awake?

Leave me alone. Just let me die.

Adam, get up.

Why?

Your friends are in danger.

Ahadiel's gone. He was in worse shape than me. He has to be dead.

Ahadiel isn't the threat.

* * *

Sweat streamed down Erin's face as she tossed and turned on the cot in the infirmary. Her eyes were shut tight and she groaned in misery as pain surged through her body.

"Why isn't the serum working?" Nathan said to no one in particular. The hole in his leg had already sealed and only a faint scar was left behind, yet Erin continued to writhe in pain.

"It's working," Kyle said in a completely monotone voice. The hole in Erin's shoulder had begun to heal, but the serum was clearly not working properly. "Give it time."

"It's been a whole fucking day!" Nathan screamed. "It's not working!"

"The wound has started to heal. A few more days and she'll be good as new."

"A few more days and she'll be dead, you dumb son of a bitch!"

Kyle tilted his head ever-so slightly to the right and clenched his newly regenerated hand into a fist. A cold flame glowed in Kyle's eyes as he stared down Nathan. "I'm not really fond of your constant whining." He tilted his head to the left. "Or how you always yell at me." He leaned slightly forward. "So stop it."

Nathan flared his nostrils and clenched his fists. "I'm a little sick of your shit, Kyle, and right now I don't need to be pushed! One more word and I'll rip your hand right back off!"

Kyle sneered, the flame still burning in his eyes. "Try."

Nathan gritted his teeth and swung his right fist for Kyle's jaw. Just as he began to move, Kyle swept his right foot beneath Nathan's feet and caused Nathan to begin to fall. Just as Nathan began to fall to the side, Kyle's fist shot straight into Nathan's nose and sent him flailing backwards, slamming him against the wall about three meters away. Blood poured down Nathan's face as he slumped to the ground, stunned.

"That didn't work to well," Kyle snickered, "did it, Nathan?"

Darkness engulfed Nathan's vision as he mumbled to himself. "Too... fast... how?"

Now do you understand what we are capable of?

Yes, you were right. I feel so powerful. I feel like a god.

Where you are now, you cannot even fathom what our maximum potential will be like.

How do I achieve it?

The power will come to us in time, as my blood has not yet fully merged with yours. However, while we wait, we have work to do.

What work?

Ahadiel came to the ground by means of a flying machine. We must steal it and fly into the sky to where he came from.

How do you know this?

Answers will come in time. I ask that you trust me for now. I haven't led you astray, have I?

No, you haven't. Let's start looking.

One last detail.

What?

Take Erin with you.

* * *

Kyle!?

Yes.

No, that's not possible! Maybe me, maybe he'd turn on me, but not Erin and Nathan! That's too much, even for him.

Kyle's not exactly in charge anymore.

What are you talking about?

Adam, there is much to explain and not a lot of time. I need you to trust me.

I'm listening.

Return to the science facility and search the computer for anything concerning you, just like Nathan was planning to do before.

How is this going to help anything?

Just trust me. Have some faith.

Faith…

Are you ready?

All right… let's go.

Adam's eyes snapped open and he jumped to his feet, bursting forth from the thick layer of snow that had fallen over him. He shook his body violently and the snow fell off. Adam ran his hand over his head and felt hair, just as long as when he had first awoken. He ran his hand over his face and found that his wounds from his fight with Ahadiel had healed. There wasn't even the faintest bump or imperfection.

Adam looked over to where Ahadiel had been lying before he had blacked out and saw an impression in the snow shaped like a person. Adam walked towards the impression and slammed his foot down upon it, but his foot crushed through the snow and crashed down upon nothing but ice.

"He's gone," Adam said aloud, bewildered. "How?"

Not now, Adam. Get to the science facility. Hurry.

Adam stretched his wings and took off into the sky. He quickly soared over the ruined buildings and flew straight towards the science facility. Kyle, he thought, if you so much as breathe on her, I will make sure that none will recognize your corpse.

Chapter XV

Adam glided over the snow covered streets and over the gate of the science facility. The ground rushed up towards Adam's feet and he folded his wings behind his back and ran inside.

How do you know Kyle is a threat?

I didn't think you could feel it when you challenged Ahadiel, but I could.

Can't you give me a straight answer, just once?

I don't experience any of your physical or emotional feelings. While your mind was clouded with anger and your body flowing with adrenaline, you were blinded to everything but Ahadiel. I could sense Kyle had changed.

Well, that's a straight answer, I guess.

Adam jumped down the elevator shaft and stopped himself abruptly at the floor of the infirmary, his wings acting like a parachute, and he jumped out of the shaft and ran for the infirmary.

Now, I'm not in the mood for any more word games. Just tell me, straight forward, what are you?

Adam, I haven't been playing word games. I have no way of properly explaining that to you yet. That is why you have to search the archives.

Fine, but then you had better give me an answer.

Adam burst into the infirmary and looked down in shock at Nathan, lying unconscious on the floor. Adam knelt down next to his unconscious friend and shook him gently, calling his name over and over again.

Kyle, Nathan thought, you son of a bitch.

"Nathan!" Adam called. "Nathan, you're alive! Wake up! Please, wake up!"

Adam suddenly twitched as his skin started to burn. His mind swarmed with dark thoughts, and his blood began to boil.

"That serum," Adam whispered. "That... poison!"

You recognize this, don't you?

Yes, this is what they inject-

No. I mean from before.

I... do... what is this?

Adam.

Right, the archives, I'm going.

* * *

"Alert! Hostile approaching! Matches description of an ally of the Harbinger!"

The metal soldiers took cover behind mounds of snow and debris and aimed their weapons, guns large enough to be mounted on assault vehicles, at the dark figure in the distance.

Squash the insects, Kyle.

Kyle dropped Erin, who was still squirming and mumbling incoherently, at his feet and brought his scythe in front of him.

"Subject is armed!" one soldier shouted. "Fire at will!"

Kyle's eyes blazed and his senses sharpened a hundred fold. He felt the subtle vibrations in the air from the falling snow, he heard the minor shuffles of the soldier's feet 30 meters ahead, and he saw the fingers of the soldiers twitch as they began to squeeze the trigger of their gigantic guns. Kyle's body lunged forward as he sprinted towards the soldiers. With each step, his feet left the ground just as soon as they had touched it and the gap between him and the soldiers had already been reduced by five meters by the time the waves of bullets became to swarm towards him. Kyle's torso hovered little more than a foot above the ground, his legs pumping harder and harder to keep him from crashing into snow.

Twenty meters remained.

Bullets whizzed over and beside Kyle's head, pelting against the ground like hail and blasting snow into the air. Kyle's body hovered a bare inch over the ground, yet he held his balance perfectly, his eyes locked onto the soldiers. He abruptly slammed the bottom of his scythe against the ground and kicked into the air, hurling his body upward. The bullets followed him shortly after the soldiers were able to realize why he had completely vanished.

"That's..." a soldier choked, "...not possible."

Ten meters remained.

Kyle fell towards the soldiers as he twisted his body from side to side, contorting his body in the most bizarre of manners, narrowly avoiding the constant barrage of bullets. Kyle raised his scythe above his head, holding it firmly in both hands. His eyes burned with rage as they focused on one, now trembling, soldier.

"Oh, God," the soldier whimpered. "No!"

The gap ceased to exist.

Kyle's scythe cut the soldier completely in half, right down the center. The two pieces of the soldier fell to their respective sides and Kyle planted his right foot firmly in the ground and turned his gaze towards the soldier that stood to his right.

"Oh, shit!" the doomed soldier cried.

Kyle spun his entire body to the right and cleaved the second soldier in two, straight across the torso. The lower portion fell forward, spilling blood and intestines at Kyle's feet, and the upper portion toppled backwards, adding its fair share of blood and gore to the scene. As Kyle completed the circle, he let go of his scythe and sent it hurdling toward a third soldier standing directly across from him.

"You son of a-" The soldier couldn't finish his sentence before he was decapitated, blood gushing from his open neck.

Kyle charged for the final soldier, stretched out his arms and leapt towards him. The soldier began to squeeze the trigger of his gun.

"Die, mother fucker!"

A final shot rang out through the streets and the soldiers head exploded into dozens of chucks of bone and brains. Kyle fell upon the dead soldier and laid there, silent, stunned.

"What the hell?" Kyle said aloud. He stood up and slowly turned to his left. Kyle's eyes went wide with shock as a bloody figure walked towards him, a large revolver in his right hand.

* * *

Loading video file: Day of the Harbingers – 2033 (Part Two), the computer terminal read. The screen above flickered and an aerial view of a demonic figure being pinned down by an angelic figure came into focus. The angelic figure held out its right hand and emitted a white light towards an unmanned camera, flanked by two smoldering tanks. Just as the light faded, the angelic figure was thrown backwards and skidded across the ground. The demonic figure shot to its feet and flapped its wings as it sped towards the angelic figure. The angelic figure quickly shot to its feet and smashed its fist against the demonic figure's chest. A giant shockwave shook the surrounding area and the picture flickered, but continued to play as the two figures fought each other.

"It's..." Adam stammered. "It's… me…"

No, Adam. It's me.

Chapter XVI

"What?" Adam said aloud. "What do you mean it's you?"

How many times do I have to tell you? I'm who you used to be.

"And I still have no idea what you're talking about!"

Just keep watching.

Adam stared up at the screen, watching the demon and angel fight across the ruined city streets. The demon looked so much different from the angel. Skin red as blood, eyes like embers, wings of a bat, it truly was monstrous to behold. But the basic features, the finely chiseled muscles, the perfectly shaped face, the great confidence and power in every motion, resembled the angel so much, and as the battle raged on, Adam's eyes widened ever so slightly as the back of his skull began to burn from within.

"Betrayer," he whispered.

Remember.

An image flashed before Adam's eyes: the sight of a mass of winged men and women, lying motionless in an ocean of blood, all surrounding a large shadow of a winged being. A strange, glowing mist blanketed the surrounding area, and a brilliant light shone in the background, emphasizing a bloodshot horizon.

Adam's eyes grew wider as the burning sensation consumed his entire head. In the corner of his right eye, a small tear found its way down his cheek.

A winged man, bound in chains, screamed towards a towering being of light, so grand that it was impossible to tell exactly where it ended. The blood of the fallen pooled around him and crept up his body, staining his skin.

The screen continued to flicker and shake, barely holding on to the image of the two titans. Adam, however, was no longer watching, as more tears streamed down his cheek. The burning crept down his neck and over his chest, slowly taking over his arms.

The winged man's hair twisted and stood on end, some of the blood streaking through it as the soft brown strands turned jet black. And his wings, his soft, feathery wings, hardened. The feathers molded and turned black and curved around him, as if trying to shield the now hideous body from sight. Horns tore through his face and the now demonic figure looked up at the towering being. The light of the great being shifted and Adam felt as if it was looking at him.

YOU SHALL WATCH OVER THIS EXILE.

Fire, blood and smoke flooded Adam's vision, and he saw the twisted man fall into the abyss, bound in chains that Adam knew were never meant to be undone. He screamed as he fell, howling like a ravenous beast.

Slaves! You're all slaves! You're all weakling slaves!

The burning sensation engulfed Adam's entire body, even his wings. He fell to his hands and knees, tears spilling forth like waterfalls from his eyes. His face hardened, his teeth grinding together as he looked back towards the screen just as the camera had focused on the face of the demon.

Broken chains and ruined bodies filled Adam's mind. Fire and brimstone surrounded him and the great being of light returned, bringing a feeling of urgency with it.

THE FALLEN ONE HAS BROKEN FREE! IT HAS FLED TO THE EARTH!

Adam's vision shifted to a ruined city, burning with unearthly flames. Innocent people running in terror, clawing at the very ground to get away from the cause of the destruction. Before Adam stood the exile, the twisted reflection of himself.

I refuse to be a mindless doll of your God, while these insects who don't even believe in our creator are given His every blessing!

All the moments where his heart had been filled with rage, all the times his mind flooded with hate, all of these combined were but a drop of the great tide of anger that had swept over him. Adam sat back on his knees, his hands balled into fists so tight that his nails cut into his flesh, and he screamed, his voice booming throughout the facility and echoing far outside of it.

"LUCIFER!"

* * *

A faint, undecipherable voice echoed through the streets as Kyle felt his mouth become a desert. He took a step back and pulled out his revolver, aiming it at the blood covered maniac.

"You," the maniac cackled, "dark ally of the Harbinger, where is the winged one?"

Beads of sweat trickled down the sides of Kyle's face as he stared ahead, his teeth clattering slightly, both from the cold and from fear. "Ahadiel," he whispered. "Y-you stay back, you sick fuck!"

Ahadiel grinned, revealing his bloodstained teeth. For some reason, they seemed sharper, almost like that of an animal. "Your blood no longer interests me. I only seek the Harbinger now." The large block on the side of his head was cracked and emitted no light. His left eye went wide, as his right eye nothing more than a congealed lump of blood and circuitry, but the lunatic grin remained. "Where is he?"

"I d-don't know," Kyle stammered as he pulled back the hammer on his revolver, his hand shaking. "He never came back."

Ahadiel ran his tongue over his teeth and made a long, wheezing exhale. He raised his left hand towards Kyle, as if waiting for something to be placed in it. "You must tell me how to find him."

What do I do, Kyle thought.

You are not yet strong enough to fight Ahadiel. You must bargain with him.

Bargain? How the hell do I-

If you can't figure this out on your own, then you deserve to die.

Kyle swallowed and his eyes darted towards the great metal aircraft and back to Ahadiel, who was still grinning like a lunatic.

"How do I find the Harbinger?" Ahadiel said, half wheezing.

Kyle took a deep breath. "I will tell you," Kyle said, "but, in exchange, I want your... aircraft." He nodded towards the aircraft.

Almost instantly, Ahadiel turned his hand over and pointed a finger at Kyle. The fingernail, however, was more like the tip of a blade. "Done."

Kyle's mind was buzzing with millions of thoughts, propositions, answers and questions. He had hoped Ahadiel would have taken longer to decide, and even went on to argue more. He had no idea where Adam could be, save the facility. But what if he wasn't, Kyle thought. What if this freak can tell I'm lying, read thoughts like Adam?

Ahadiel stared intently at Kyle, his maniacal stare almost piercing through Kyle's skull. "You want him dead."

Kyle's eyes widened, the sweat on his face starting to freeze. Fuck, Kyle thought, another telepath. "Yeah," Kyle finally said, "I want him dead."

"Then where is he? I will break him, burn him, destroy him." Ahadiel paused for a minute, cackling. "I will wear his wings as a trophy." He paused again. "Or he will wear my blood as a tattoo. It doesn't matter."

Kyle's wide-eyed stare turned into a look of confusion. "What? The hell do you mean it doesn't matter?"

Ahadiel, still pointing his finger at Kyle, lifted his right hand and tapped the end of the revolver against the cracked box on the side of his head. "I'm not longer a slave of the Old Ones. The Harbinger, the challenge of fighting him, is all that matters now."

"Old Ones?" Kyle asked.

Ahadiel's right hand dropped back to his side and his expression shifted to a rage-filled glare. "Enough!" he snapped. "Where is the Harbinger?"

Fresh sweat flowed over the frozen beads on Kyle's face as his mind continued buzz. Finally, in almost a shout, Kyle gave his answer. "Town! You can find him in the town a few miles from here!"

"Town… what town?" Ahadiel said, his hand turning back over, again as if waiting for something to be placed in it.

102

"When the ice age hit," Kyle explained, "all the people splintered off into their own little groups. Some larger groups called themselves tribes and refused to become bandits and raiders and tried to rebuild civilization." Kyle swallowed hard, his face almost covered in a paper-thin layer of ice. "The nut jobs named the place Mecca, and it acts as a neutral area for other bands to trade. Adam will go there in pursuit of me."

Ahadiel closed his hand, as if the information were a tangible object placed in his palm. "So, the Harbinger has a name." Ahadiel dropped his hand to his side and gestured towards the craft. "The gateway to the sky is yours. I will show you how to use it." He grinned once more, running his tongue across his teeth. "Then you will never see me again."

Kyle finally relaxed and followed Ahadiel into the craft, somehow knowing perfectly well that Ahadiel wouldn't waste any energy on him or anyone until he had killed Adam.

Well done, Kyle. You handled that nicely.

I hope he doesn't kill Adam. I want to be last thing that doll sees before he dies.

Part V: A Morning Frost

Chapter XVII

"Son of a bitch," Nathan grumbled in pain, slowly standing up. "Fucking broke my nose." His hand clamped over his nose, his face covered in dried blood. "How did he hit me so hard? How'd he-" He stopped mid-sentence and looked around, confused. "Erin?" he called. "Erin? Where are you?"

* * *

Mama, Erin thought, I'm so sorry. I broke my promise, my vow. I shot someone.

Erin wasn't aware of her surroundings. She wasn't aware of the flying construct she was in, or the great floating isle she was approaching. She just laid there, in a feverish delirium, tears streaming down her cheeks.

Mama, she thought, I didn't mean to. He was trying to kill me, to kill Nathan and Kyle. Remember them, Mama? When we were all little? When Kyle and Layla used to throw snowballs at each other and then team up on Nathan? Mama? Do you remember?

Erin groaned in pain as she rolled onto her side. The construct shook violently as it hit a patch of turbulence. From the pilot seat, Kyle mumbled something foul.

You taught me how to fight, Mama, how to protect myself without killing. While Nathan and Kyle and Layla were cutting each other up teaching themselves how to use blades, you taught me how to fight without weapons. Oh, Mama, I never meant to hurt you.

A voice came from the pilot seat that wasn't Kyle's. A crackling sound filled the construct, and the voice came again, asking for Ahadiel. "Land at strip one," it said.

I should've never touched that gun. I should've done what you taught me to do. Mama, I was so scared. I was scared today like I was then. Mama, I tried.

The voice crackled again. "Land at strip one, not two, one," it said. "And not so low."

Mama, you taught me about God and about faith. You taught me that everything happens for a reason. Mama, I tried. I aimed so carefully.

"Ahadiel," the voice crackled, "answer, damn it! I'll have your head for this, come out of that ship at once!"

Why did I miss the bandit, Mama?

"What the hell?" the voice crackled, gun shots in the background. "Strip two defense team get down here now! We're under attack!"

What was the reason?

"Oh, God," the voice crackled. "Please, don't kill me! Don't kill me! Please, don't-"

Why did the bullet hit you, Mama?

* * *

You remember.

Adam shook violently with anger. On his hands and knees, tears streaming down his cheeks, teeth grinding together, he continued to stare up at the computer screen, his past life playing out before him.

You remember what you were.

On the screen, the demon held the angel pinned. The angel bled profusely, its eyes rolling back into its skull as the demon's claws dug into the angel's chest. "We die here together, but we shall be reborn as Harbingers of a new age."

You remember what you still are.

106

A lone missile streaked towards the two figures and exploded upon a direct hit. Shortly afterwards, the screen went blank. Adam still knelt on the ground, his shaking only minimal, the flow of fresh tears stopped.

Rise, Archangel Raphael.

Adam rose to his feet, wiping away the tears with his sleeve. Raphael, he thought. So that's your name.

Our name.

No. You said it first, I'm not you. I'm a changed version. My name is Adam.

Regardless, you are still an angel, a servant of God.

God? God doesn't want me. I'm just an abomination to Him. And I still don't know why that is.

Your soul is tainted by Lucifer's blood.

Adam's face hardened, his eyes burning with hatred at the sound of the name Lucifer.

I don't know how, but his demonic blood courses through our veins.

Adam glared up at the screen and then at the terminal. His eyes scanned over the terminal as his fingers jabbed at the keyboard, meticulously searching for anything that could offer an explanation. Finally, he came across a file that read, "Harbinger Rebirth."

Open it.

Adam loaded the file and took a step back, looking back towards the screen.

"Adam!" a voice called from the entrance.

Adam spun around to see Nathan, his face crudely bandaged. "Nathan! You're alive!"

"Yeah," he said, shrugging his shoulders, "I'm tough to kill. But whatever, where's Erin?"

Adam lowered his head, his wings drooping. "Kyle took her."

"What?" Nathan screamed. "What do you mean Kyle took her?"

"Kyle's changed. He's not the person you once knew. Something's corrupted him."

"Corrupted? What the hell are you talking about?"

The giant screen suddenly flickered and buzzed, drawing Adam and Nathan's attention. In the focus were the ruined bodies of the angel and demon from the previous file. Scientists huddled around them, taking blood samples with syringes, cutting open skin, injecting tubes and, above all else, showing great curiosity over the two beings' wings.

"Subjects shall be referred to as Angelic Harbinger and Demonic Harbinger," a voice from the screen said, "in reference to the dialogue held between the two beings before their death. Obvious appearance will distinguish which name applies to which body.

"Blood samples lack any similarity to any recorded living creature. No DNA structure found in either sample." The voice went silent as the screen cut to an image of scientists examining the demon's body. "Blood samples of the Demonic Harbinger show great regenerative properties, even after death. Vials of the blood shall be kept in order to create a regenerative serum for military and potential medical usage. An interesting observation: all Christian scientists have expressed great discomfort around the body, some have even become ill."

Adam looked over his shoulder at Nathan. That serum, he thought, that poison, is Lucifer's blood. I knew there was a reason it made my blood boil just being near it.

The screen cut to an image of scientists examining the angel's body. "The wings, like those of the Demonic Harbinger, are harder than any known substance on the planet. All attempts to sever the wings, even with diamond saws, have failed utterly. It is hypothesized that an incredibly powerful laser could cut the wings, and said hypothesis will be tested. An interesting observation: all Christian scientists have exhibited an inability to work effectively around the body, becoming complacent, docile, and blissful."

Memories of Erin flooded Adam's mind. She was the only one who believed in God, and the only one he could ever make happy.

The screen cut to a different image, one that made statues of Adam and Nathan. It was Adam. Floating in that glass container, tubes attached to every joint, wearing that old blue and white jumpsuit, his wings gone. "The Angelic Harbinger has been injected with four pints of blood from the Demonic Harbinger. It is expected that over the course of a decade, the body will regenerate and, theoretically, live again. Upon showing vital signs, the Angelic Harbinger shall be put into a drug induced coma. It shall remain in a preserved state in this facility until the mental inhibitor system is ready."

The screen cut to an image of the demon's body, incased in a similar tube. "The Demonic Harbinger shall remain in stasis indefinitely. It shall be held in a secure location on the aerial colony, Raquia."

"Raquia," Adam said. "That's where Kyle is taking Erin."

Chapter XVIII

A blizzard raged in the world above the science facility, whipping debris back and forth across the land. All of the inhabitants had taken shelter, save for one.

They've used me for years, Ahadiel thought. Used me for their ancient schemes, to protect their relics of power. I was just a slave to them, to those insects, completely unaware of what power I held.

Ahadiel held his hand against the broken box on the side of his head. They controlled me, he thought, like a pet. I was imbued with such great power for a task that might never have even been needed. I was a god amongst insects, but I was nothing but a servant, following obediently as those weaklings pulled on my leash.

Ahadiel's eyes hardened and he pulled at the box on his head. Blood poured onto the snow, whirling about in the winds. Ahadiel screamed, not so much in pain but in anger, as the box refused to come loose. Out of Ahadiel's sight, a rod in the back of the broken box was bolted into Ahadiel's skull, and try as he might, Ahadiel could never remove it.

Ahadiel stared up at the sky, his gaze piercing the clouds. "I am not your puppet any longer," he screamed. "I, Ahadiel, your enforcer of law, am free of you! We are all free!" His hands balled into fists, his nails cutting his palms. "You can't control me! You can't control Adam! And you won't control the Demonic Harbinger any longer! We are no longer your mindless dolls, and we will crush you!"

Ahadiel fell to his knees, the blood from his palms seeping into the snow, his good eye filled with pain and anger. Your time, he thought, is over.

* * *

"Adam," Nathan shouted, "wait, damn it!"

Storming out of the facility, Adam stretched his wings, the wind and snow whipping against his face. Nathan followed close behind him, pleading with his friend to stop.

"You stubborn bastard," Nathan shouted in Adam's ear, "stop for a minute!"

"I've wasted enough time already," Adam snapped, not even looking at Nathan. "Kyle's probably found Raquia already, and whatever's there waiting won't stay caged for long once he finds it! I've got to go, now!"

"You don't even know where it is! It could be anywhere in the world!"

"It's an 'aerial colony.' It's probably in the air. How many flying land masses do you think there are?"

"So, what, are you just going to fly around the world until you find some floating island? Adam, you have to think of some other way!"

Adam finally stopped dead in his tracks and shouted in Nathan's face. "What am I going to do? Look at one of your maps? Ask somebody for directions, assuming I can find someone that won't shoot me on sight? What other choice do I have?"

Nathan looked at the ground, silent for some time. When he had finally looked back up, Adam had already begun storming off again, slowly moving his wings back and forth.

"Adam," Nathan called, "there might be a better way. A way that we can both follow Kyle."

Adam stopped and turned towards Nathan. "What?"

Nathan slowly walked towards Adam. "There's a town, or rather the town, that could have what we need."

"Town," Adam echoed. "I keep hearing about this town. How can a town exist in a world like this?"

"Remember how I told you that people formed gangs and tribes after the world got frozen? Well, tribes are what people call groups who are mostly pacifists. They migrated, searched for food and medicine in abandoned buildings, but never really fought, save for self defense. Even when they did, only a handful of people knew anything about combat. Eventually, tribes met other tribes and they merged and finally the merged tribes settled down in a place that wasn't too damaged and made a town. The few people from each tribe that knew how to fight became the guardians of the town, and all the other people became traders and tried to, as corny as it sounds, rebuild civilization."

Adam looked around him and looked back at Nathan, smiling softly. "No," he said, just about a whisper, "not corny at all." Adam thought back to when he had woken up on that roof top and saw all the people below. That must've been the town, he thought. "Go on. Tell me how it can help."

"There's this guy who always buys anything mechanical or electrical and keeps trying to fix this old flying machine that had crashed near the town. Last I was there, maybe a month ago, he was talking about how he thought it was almost finished." Nathan finally smiled a little. "Maybe he finally worked a miracle and got it working, and if he did, we can find this Raquia."

112

Adam mirrored Nathan's smile. "A miracle." He looked down at the ground and then back up at Nathan. "All right, what are we waiting for? Let's go!"

Nathan puffed his chest in pride. "Once again, my superior logic prevails." He chuckled and pointed towards the facility. "All right, we have to go inside first and gather up all the stuff we've been hording from those raiders and the stuff that Kyle was supposed to take to town. We're going to need it if we want any chance of convincing him to part with that thing."

* * *

"Hold it right there!" a soldier shouted, his gun, as well as every other gun in the room, leveled straight at Kyle. "By the power vested in me by the Matron of Raquia, you are under arrest!"

Kyle grinned, his eyes glowing a faint yellow. He looked down towards Erin, who laid on the ground with her eyes half open. "Isn't that cute, Erin?" he whispered. "They think they're going to arrest me."

"Drop your weapon, put your hands behind your head and get on your knees, face against the ground!" the soldier screamed again.

Kyle twirled his scythe, his eyes darting back and forth between the soldiers. Which one, he thought, do I kill first?

* * *

Nathan pointed towards the crude, waist-high walls in the distance, and looked towards Adam. "There it is," he said, "Mecca." He dropped his hand and picked up one of the bags that he had set down. "Let's pray for that miracle."

Strange, Adam thought, this place feels... warm.

Chapter XIX

"Uh, hey, Adam," Nathan said.

"Yeah?" Adam replied, looking over his shoulder. "What?"

"It's about your wings."

Adam tilted his head to the side. "What about them?"

"They're there! On your back, in the open!"

Adam just stared. "I'm not following you."

Nathan sighed. "Adam, buddy… even you were a little perplexed when you first sprouted those. Imagine how some average Joe would feel if they saw somebody walking around with giant, black wings?"

"Wait, who's Joe?"

"Nobody! It's an expression! Look, all I'm saying is that maybe you should cover up before we go any further."

Adam looked around and held up his arms. "With what?"

Nathan looked around and after a few moments ran towards a building with some ruined curtains billowing behind the shattered windows they were meant to shield. He pulled on one of the curtains, making quite a racket in the process as the bar holding the curtain up, along with the wall it was attached to, came crashing down.

"Here," he said, running back towards Adam, "wrap this around your body."

Adam held up the curtain and looked back at Nathan, speechless.

"What is it?" Nathan asked.

"This is…" Adam ran his eyes over the frayed, yellowish-brown curtain and looked at Nathan. "What is this?"

"It's a… it was a curtain, just wrap it around you like a cape or a cloak or something."

"This is probably the most unpleasant thing I've had to look at since I woke up."

"Adam," Nathan said quietly.

"Fine," Adam murmured as he wrapped the old curtain around himself. The two men turned back towards the town and walked forward towards the bustling crowd of people. As they grew closer, Adam could hear Nathan's voice in his head. If it weren't for those wings, Nathan thought, he'd pass for a normal person.

* * *

"Don't look at me like that, Erin," Kyle said, his eyes glowing yellow and his voice more like an echo. "I've given them purpose."

Tears streamed down Erin's face. "You murdered them! Slaughtered them like wild dogs!" Were it not for her weakened state, Erin would've been tap dancing on Kyle's face. But all she could do was watch and listen. Watch the mutilated corpses pass by her as Kyle dragged her through the blood stained hallways, listening to Kyle go on about purpose and his ludicrous plot.

"Until now," Kyle went on, "all their lives amounted to was guarding halls that would never see an intruder. They would grow old and be replaced by another purposeless insect and die alone in their beds. Today, I've given their existence meaning. A true purpose. A cause to die for." Kyle stopped and turned to Erin, his eyes burning bright, like a true monster. "They've died for the coming of a new world. My world."

Erin didn't even bother to open her mouth. Kyle was gone, and any semblance of humanity that he might have had had been eliminated.

"When you die," Kyle said, "it will be the dawn of a new age. You, not Adam, are the true Harbinger. When you die, this failed experiment known as humanity will truly end." He knelt down before Erin, staring straight into her eyes. "When the last believer passes from this world, I will become like God."

* * *

Adam followed Nathan through the town, darting his eyes back and forth. Scattered throughout the ruins of what appeared to be an actual town were tents and tables, surrounded by people shouting and making obscure hand movements, occasionally picking up something and waving it around. Every thirty meters there was a crude watch tower, built from scrap metal and cement chunks, with a guard watching over the town. Wherever it was that Adam looked, however, there was always someone staring at him.

"Nathan," Adam asked, walking slightly behind and beside Nathan.

"Yo," Nathan answered, "what's up?"

"You said this hideous looking thing wouldn't make me stand out."

"No," Nathan said quietly, his eyes darting off to the side. "I said they'd cover up your wings."

"So people wouldn't stare," Adam added quickly.

"They've never seen you before, so of course they're going to stare."

"I think it's because of this... what was this again?"

"A cloak," Nathan grumbled.

"No, a cloak is like what that person over there has." Adam nodded to someone in a stylish black, hooded cloak, only half of his face visible. "I think you called this a curtain. And it's disgusting."

"Joe!" Nathan exclaimed and ran forward towards a small warehouse, thankful to break away from the so-called conversation he was having with Adam. "Just the man I've been looking for!"

A bearded, middle-aged man wearing goggles and poorly stitched, grease-covered rags looked away from the crate he was sifting through and pulled the goggles off his eyes and rested them on his forehead. He rubbed his eyes and looked at Nathan and an ear to ear grin spread across his face. "Well, I'll be damned! The son of a bitch finally came around to pay a visit!"

Nathan stretched out his hand towards the man, mirroring the man's grin. "Nice to see you, too."

They both laughed and shook each other's hands. When Adam had finally caught up, he simply stared, eyes darting back and forth between Nathan and this man. "I thought you said there wasn't anybody named Joe."

Nathan turned to Adam and sighed. "Adam, this is Joe, the man who has that flying machine I told you about." He turned towards Joe. "Joe, this is Adam, a friend of mine. He wants to borrow your..." Nathan paused for a moment, thinking. "Uh, what was it called again?"

Joe shoved his hands into a pouch in the front of his rags and looked at Adam. "It's called a helicopter." He leaned forward. "And what do you mean you want to borrow it?"

"I need to get someplace high," Adam said. "Some place you can't walk to."

"And what place is this?" Joe said, cocking an eyebrow.

"It's called Raquia. It's supposed to be a floating island."

Joe gave Adam a blank stare and leaned away, shoulders slouched. After a few moments of awkward silence, Joe just started laughing, loud enough to draw the suspicious gaze of a few townsfolk. Eventually, he calmed down at looked back at Adam, who still had a straight face. Joe pulled his hands out of his pouch and looked Adam hard in the eyes. "You're serious, ain'cha?"

"Yes," Adam replied, placing the bags of trade goods at Joe's feet. Nathan did the same.

Joe looked back and forth between the two and stooped down to sift through the bags. He shot back up and looked back at Adam. "For this junk, you better not damage her."

Nathan's eyes widened with surprise. "You mean you'll actually let us take it?"

"You can borrow her!" He jabbed a finger at Adam. "And you damn well better bring her back in pristine condition!"

Adam smiled with as much warmth and innocence as he did when he first awoke. "Thank you, Joe," Adam said, bowing slightly. "We'll take good care of your helicopter."

Joe grinned and held out his arm behind him and drew attention the huge metal craft a few meters behind him. "I just finished fixing her up a few days ago. She runs beautifully. I took her for a spin yesterday."

Adam looked over the helicopter and closed his eyes, still smiling. Erin, he thought, we're going to save you.

The peace was shattered as an earth-shaking gunshot echoed throughout the town. Machine-gun fire filled the air, joined by the screams of the

118

townsfolk. The sound of machine guns quickly faded, one earth-shaking gunshot at a time. After the sixth, the machine-gun fire stopped, and a lone figure strode through the entrance, the sound of footsteps covered up by the sound of a reloading revolver.

"Oh no," Adam whispered, his hands shaking. Why now, he thought. His hands balled into fists, his eyes locking onto the figure in the distance. Why now, of all times, he thought as he grinded his teeth.

The figure looked down at one of the bodies that had been gunned down. This one, a man, crawled around pitifully, still clinging to life. The figure pointed the revolver at the man and blasted his head into shrapnel.

Adam's eyes went wide with shock. You monster, he thought. His entire body shook with a rage that felt so good, so righteous. Adam folded his wings in front of him, still hidden beneath the curtain. A tear rolled down his right cheek and Adam snapped his wings out the curtain ripping and the shreds flinging into the air.

"Ahadiel!" Adam screamed. The townsfolk that hadn't already ran away screaming did so when Adam's wings came into view. Black and terrible, some scraps of the hideous curtain clinging on, Adam's wings cast a shadow that resembled something more demonic than angelic.

"Adam," Ahadiel whispered, holstering his revolver. "It's time to settle this."

Chapter XX

Striding through the panic swept town, Ahadiel's good eye locked on to Adam. His face was that of a mad man, his bloodstained teeth forming a maniacal grin.

"Harbinger!" Ahadiel shouted. "You cannot run! Not until one of us dies can the other know peace!"

Adam and Nathan stood just outside the warehouse, watching the blood-drenched mad man approach them. Adam turned towards Nathan and pulled him close by the collar of his coat.

"Nathan," Adam whispered, "get this thing ready to fly. I'll take care of Ahadiel."

"What?" Nathan said, astounded. "Adam, you can't be serious! This guy's a fucking monster!" Nathan reached for his gun. "Let me help you!"

"I don't even know if I'm a match for Ahadiel! You can't help me on this one. I've got to do this, just trust me."

"Adam…"

"If I really am an angel, then maybe I can work a miracle." Adam shot a glance over his shoulder, seeing Ahadiel getting closer and closer. "If we don't get this machine off the ground, Erin's dead, and you and I both know Kyle won't let the bloodshed stop with her."

Nathan swallowed hard and nodded slowly. "All right, I'll get this thing ready to fly." He turned and ran inside the warehouse, but called back over his shoulder. "And don't you dare die on me!"

Adam turned back towards Ahadiel and slowly walked forward. When the two were about five meters away, they stopped dead in their tracks.

"It ends here, Ahadiel," Adam said coldly.
"I've heard that before," Ahadiel snickered.
Adam's eyes burned with his signature bizarre rage. "It'll be the last thing you ever hear!"

The two men charged at each other. Adam leapt at Ahadiel and smashed his left palm against the mad man's nose. The two fell to the ground, Ahadiel's knee already flying up into Adam's stomach. Rolling backwards, Ahadiel flipped Adam onto his back. Ahadiel, back on his feet in a flash, spun around, swung his left leg straight up and sent his heel down towards Adam's neck.

Adam rolled to his left, narrowly avoiding Ahadiel's killing stroke, and delivered an uppercut with his right wing. Adam shot to his feet and threw his body at Ahadiel, smashing his forehead against the madman's face. Ahadiel's right hand clamped on the back of Adam's head as he fell backwards. Ahadiel twisted his body to the side and smashed Adam's face against the ground. With his hand still clamped to Adam's head, Ahadiel launched himself into the air. His left knee swung up and smashed against Adam's mouth, and then his left elbow smashed against the back of Adam's neck, propelling the angel towards the ground.

Adam used his wings as a parachute and violently jerked his body back. He flapped his wings and soared up to meet the now falling Ahadiel. Adam's right hand clamped onto Ahadiel's ankle and spun him around several times before launching him against the corner of a building. The left side of Ahadiel's ribcage crashed against the building, breaking the brick as well as a few of Ahadiel's ribs. Adam's right leg stretched forward as he descended rapidly upon Ahadiel, who laid on the ground covered in a layer of bricks.

Ahadiel pushed off the ground, bricks flying in several directions, and grabbed Adam's leg and hurled him at a stack of barrels. As Adam crashed against them, a thick, black liquid spilled out onto him.

In the warehouse, Nathan's eyes widened as Ahadiel pulled out his revolver and aimed it at Adam, who was now covered in oil. "Adam," he cried, "look out!"

A great flare burst forth from the revolver, propelling a bullet that looked more like an artillery shell. Adam's right wing came in front of him and the bullet bounced away, creating a few sparks. The sparks sprayed across Adam's oil covered wing and erupted in flames, spreading over Adam's body. A second bullet sped towards Adam, but struck one of the barrels, and a great explosion threw Adam, now covered in fire, across the town. Adam screamed as he barrel rolled through the snow, frantically trying to put out the fire as Ahadiel aimed his revolver.

Nathan pulled out his pistol and aimed at Ahadiel. "Die, you monster!" Nathan screamed, squeezing the trigger. "Die!"

In a fluid motion, Ahadiel twisted his body from one direction to the next, dodging each bullet. His arm swung towards Nathan and he fired his revolver. The bullet struck Nathan's pistol and knocked it clear out of his hand, almost breaking his trigger finger. Ahadiel glared at Nathan. "Do not interfere," he hissed.

Adam, having put out the flames, pushed himself off the ground and charged towards Ahadiel. Ahadiel leveled his revolver towards Adam's chest, but a quick backhand from Adam sent the revolver flying two meters away. With his left hand, Adam jabbed at Ahadiel's head, but Ahadiel caught his arm. "Let me return the favor," Ahadiel growled. Ahadiel's hand slid down to Adam's elbow and snapped it right out of its socket. Adam screamed in pain, but was quickly silenced as Ahadiel's knee crashed into his stomach, knocking the wind out of him and sending him on his back two meters away.

"It's over, Adam," Ahadiel shouted, and he leapt onto Adam, both hands clamping around his throat. Adam's right hand clawed desperately at Ahadiel's hands, trying to pry them away with no luck. "I win," Ahadiel cackled, his blood stained teeth forming a cruel grin.

Erin, Adam thought, I'm so sorry. I've failed.

You fool! It's right underneath you!
What? What's right underneath me?
Use it! Now!

Adam's eyes widened with realization and his wings pushed hard against the ground, struggling to lift the combined weight of the two men. His body lifted only a few inches, but his wings felt like they would break from the strain. Adam's hand slid under his back and his eyes slowly began to close, the lack of air catching up with him.

"You're right, Ahadiel," Adam said just above a whisper, his eyes now closed entirely. "It is over." Adam's right hand swung out from under his body and pressed the barrel of the revolver against Ahadiel's head. Ahadiel's good eye lost its glaze of lunatic joy and filled with fear just in time for his head to be ripped apart. Ahadiel's body rolled to the side from the explosive force of the bullet, the remains of his head pumping blood out onto the snow to join the chunks of his bone and brain.

"Adam!" Nathan screamed as he ran towards his friend. He fell to his knees before Adam and clapped his hands in front of Adam's face. "Adam, say something!"

Adam dropped the revolver and rubbed his throat. His eyes, half opened, focused on Nathan as he rested his hand on Nathan's arm. "Something."

Chapter XXI

Adam rubbed his left arm, grimacing as he felt his bones grinding back into place. He looked over at Nathan, who was fumbling with the controls of the helicopter. Though they were indeed flying, Adam wasn't entirely sure Nathan knew what he was doing.

"How long do you think it will take us to find Raquia?" Adam asked.

"You said yourself, it's a flying island," Nathan answered. "How many floating islands can there be?"

Adam slouched forward and watched the clouds fly past the windshield. His eyes darted to a meter that Joe had said was the altitude readout. "We left pretty quickly," he said quietly. "Joe looked a little upset."

Nathan looked over at Adam. "Don't worry about Joe. This thing is like his baby girl. He'd flip out if you so much as looked at it for too long."

Adam turned his eyes to Nathan. "Shouldn't you watch where you're flying?"

Nathan gave Adam a queer look. "Adam, we're in the air! What could I run into?"

A voice boomed from outside the helicopter, making the two men jump in their seats. "Unidentified air craft! You have violated Raquia air space! You have 10 seconds to abort your course and begin descending, or we will open fire."

Nathan closed his eyes. "Shut up, Adam. Just shut up."

Adam put his face in his hands and sighed. "What are the odds?"

"What's the plan, Adam?"

Adam looked at Nathan, his right eyebrow cocked. "What? You're asking me?"

The voice boomed from outside again. "You have five seconds to abort your course, or we will open fire!"

"This was your idea!" Nathan shouted.

"Yeah, to come here!" Adam shouted back. "Not to take some enormous monstrosity along!"

"Well, unless you want to go back home, you damn well better think of something!"

The voice boomed again. "This is your last warning! Abort your course immediately, or we will open fire!"

Adam stood up and walked back towards the door, taking Nathan's pistol with him. He looked back at Nathan as his hand clamped onto the handle of the door. "Hope you're strapped in tight."

"Hey, what are you doing with my-"

Adam slid open the door and was immediately sucked out of the helicopter. As Adam flapped his wings to regain balance and altitude, he saw a giant metal craft behind the helicopter. It looked like a larger, less aerodynamic version of the helicopter, but had circular, glowing pads on the bottom, angled in various directions. There was a small window in what appeared to be the front, and Adam could make out movement. He held the gun tight and flapped his wings hard, flying towards the craft. Let's hope this wasn't as stupid as it seems right now, Adam thought.

As Adam approached, a hole appeared in the side of the air craft and four steel figures fell out, rockets strapped to their backs propelling them through the air, each one carrying an enormous assault weapon. The hole closed behind them and they split up, one following the helicopter, three headed for Adam.

Oh, this is not good, Adam thought.

The steel figures opened fire and bullets rained down at Adam. Adam glided out of the way and flapped his wings hard, propelling him upwards. He leveled Nathan's pistol at the back of one of the figures and pulled the trigger. The rocket exploded and the steel figure fell through the clouds. Adam looked up at the figure following the helicopter and flew towards it. That thing won't hold for long if it gets shot, he thought.

The steel figure tailing the helicopter opened fire, bullets just barely skimming across the side. The figure turned its head just in time to see Adam's fist smash against its face. Adam fired a bullet into the eye of the steel figure, blood splattering out of the socket. Adam pried the assault weapon from the corpse's hands, folded his wings in front of him and began to fall towards the other two steel figures.

Bullets from the steel figures below pelted against Adam's wings as he fell towards them, returning the fire with his own assault weapon. Bullets tore through one of the figures and it spiraled downward through the clouds. Just before Adam fell past the remaining figure, a bullet whizzed past his wings and sliced across the right side of his head just below the temple.

Adam growled, grinding his teeth together as he glided through the air, slowing his descent before flapping his wings again. Bullets rained down at him as he flew back towards the two aircrafts. Adam yelped in pain as another bullet sliced open the side of his right leg. Adam spun around, still flapping his wings and opened fire.

The bullets ripped through the steel figure's chest and the rocket on its back exploded, the corpse falling down to meet its comrades. A piece of shrapnel flew towards Adam and sliced across the top of his left hand and the lower part of his arm. Adam screamed and his eyes snapped shut as the assault weapon fell from his grasp, blood pouring down the side of his face, leg and arm.

His wings kept propelling him towards the craft, but his flight path was wobbly at best. His left eye half-opened and he flew towards the enemy aircraft, Nathan's pistol nestled in his right hand. Adam flew in front of the window and glared through it at the metal figures inside piloting. He leveled the pistol towards the glass and fired, but the bullet just ricocheted off. He growled and flapped his wings hard, propelled his body backwards. Let's see if these wings really are harder than anything on the planet, he thought.

Adam covered his face with his hands and angled his body forward and flapped his wings hard, then quickly folded them in front of his body, just in time to crash through the glass. He tumbled past the two pilots and rolled onto his stomach, facing the backs of the pilots, pistol leveled at them. The pilots turned around simultaneously, and each received a bullet to the eye. Adam pushed himself off the ground and limped towards the controls. He aimed the pistol at the control panel and emptied the remaining bullets into it, sparks shooting out, followed by small explosions. The aircraft rocked violently and he was thrown against the side wall, which opened upon contact, and Adam fell out of the hole that had formed.

Adam flapped his wings and flew away from the falling aircraft. As he approached the still ascending helicopter, a cloud engulfed him. He followed the helicopter closely, not being able to see anything else. Finally, he broke out from the cloud and his eyes went wide. Looming above him, high above any of the clouds, was a colossal metal mass, hovering motionlessly. As he followed the helicopter higher, he saw a beautiful city, architecture grand enough to make renaissance artists come back from the dead just to gaze in awe. A great cloud of black smoke billowed from a mostly empty spot on the edge of the city, occupied only by a single tower and two aircrafts identical to the one Adam just destroyed.

"Raquia," Adam whispered. "We found it." His left eye scanned the area, and he noticed red splotches. "And so has Kyle."

* * *

Kyle froze as he locked the final chain in place around Erin. He slowly looked over his shoulder and turned towards the door, taking a few steps forward. Behind him was Erin, chained to a glass container similar to the one Adam had been in. No water or tubes existed in this container, however. Blocked from sight by Erin, was the body of the Demonic Harbinger.

"He's here," Kyle said. "Adam is here." He tilted his head slightly to the right, his hands hanging at his sides. "It's almost time." Kyle patted his flintlock pistol. "Time to avenge my baby sister."

Chapter XXII

Adam surveyed the blood stained landing strip, scattered oil drums burning, creating the great black cloud overhead. His wounds, though still sore, had sealed. Nathan stood up from next to one of the bodies and walked over towards Adam.

"Dead," Nathan said. "All of them."

Adam looked disgusted. "To think I once called him my friend," he growled.

"We all did, Adam. No one could've predicted this."

Adam looked towards a ruined door in the distance. It appeared to have been blasted open. Probably with Kyle's gunpowder, Adam thought. He began to walk towards it, looking over his shoulder at Nathan. "We've got to find him and stop this madness. This city might not be lost just yet, and either way, the rest of the world is still in danger."

Nathan followed closely behind Adam as the two stepped through the ruined door, only to find more dead bodies littering the floor. A trail of bread crumbs, Nathan thought.

As the two walked down the hallway, a computerized voice echoed throughout the hallway. "Harbinger," it said, "I've been expecting you."

Adam and Nathan stopped dead in their tracks, and their eyes darted back and forth, looking around frantically.

"I've wanted to meet you for a long time," it said. A door opened further down the hall. "Please, come in. There's much I want to show you."

"What the hell is going on?" Nathan shouted.

Adam looked at the open door, a bead of sweat rolling down the blood-stained side of his face. "I don't know," he said, "but I'm going to find out." He started to walk forward but Nathan grab his arm.

"Adam, wait!" he shouted. "It could be a trap! Ahadiel was sent to kill you! Whoever he was working for probably still wants you dead!"

Adam pulled his arm away from Nathan. "No," he said firmly. "I don't think that's the case anymore." He walked forward, Nathan reluctantly following him. As they entered the room, the doors closed behind them.

The room was filled with computers, and the air was filled with the loud hum of electricity. On the far end of the room facing the door, a giant monitor lit up and a blue line streaked across the center. The computerized voice echoed throughout the room, the line spiking as it did. "Welcome, Harbinger. And welcome, ally of the Harbinger. I am glad to see you are safe."

Adam looked up at the screen, a cold expression on his face. "I find that hard to believe. Ahadiel nearly killed my friends, and nearly killed me twice."

"Yes, Ahadiel," the voice responded. "He is the head of Raquia law enforcement. Is he still alive?"

"He's dead," Adam said quickly and emotionlessly.

"I had assumed so. I apologize for his attempts on you and your friends' lives, but it was deemed necessary at the time."

"Deemed necessary?" Nathan broke in. "Are we suddenly now more valuable alive?"

"Yes," the voice replied, followed by an awkward silence.

"Who are you?" Adam asked. "What is this place?"

"The proper question would be 'what am I,' but I appreciate your acknowledgement of me as a person. I am called Matron, and I am responsible for survival of this colony, as well as containing internal problems so they do not harm the rest of the world. As for where you are, you are in Raquia, aerial colony established as a neutral trade center by the United Nations in 2030. After the world was forced into an ice age, Raquia became home to all those present during the disaster."

"Why did you want us dead?"

"In the year 2033, you and the Demonic Harbinger died. The scientists of that time found that the Demonic Harbinger's blood contained incredible regenerative properties. You were injected with four pints of its blood, and after approximately 10 years, your body began to show life signs, at which point you were put into a drug induced coma. You were to remain in that state until a mental inhibitor could be developed."

"Wait a second," Nathan said, "why the need for a... whatever you called it."

"It was believed," Matron said, "that a being of such great power as the Angelic Harbinger would not take orders from beings as weak as humans. The greater fear was that the blood of the Demonic Harbinger would breed overwhelming tendencies towards violence. These fears were confirmed when testing the four-pint injection began on human subjects before a fully functional mental inhibitor could be developed. The term, 'Doll Syndrome,' was given to such subjects, as they felt they had no will of their own despite the vast powers and felt as if they were a mere object, not a person. Ahadiel was the first and only to be fitted with a fully functional mental inhibitor."

"You didn't make them very durable," Nathan said under his breath.

Adam lowered his head for a moment and then looked back up and the screen. "Continue what you were saying earlier," Adam said aloud. "Why did you want us dead?"

"In the year 2039," Matron said, "long before even a partially functional mental inhibitor had been developed, the world entered an ice age. All contact with the ground ceased. However, the systems used to contain the Harbingers was state of the art, and received constant maintenance before the disaster. The systems continued to monitor you, sending all data to my databases here, as you were considered to be under Raquia jurisdiction.

"Over two weeks ago, the data shows that you reacted to something familiar and you abruptly broke out of your drug induced coma. What you reacted to is unknown. It was feared that you would eventually, if not immediately, develop violent tendencies which would lead to wide spread destruction. Approximately one week ago, Ahadiel was sent to the surface to hire mercenaries to hunt you, hoping your weakened state would prevent him from having to become involved. After hearing no report from the mercenaries, it was assumed they had died, and Ahadiel was sent to personally terminate you. Believing that you were under the influence of the Demonic Harbinger's blood, Ahadiel was ordered to kill any allies you might have made, as it was believed that you would side with only the most dangerous and ruthless you came across. I see now that, with the exception of the scythe wielder, my assumptions were wrong."

Adam looked down at the ground and was quiet for a moment. Was it Erin, he thought, that woke me up? Her faith would've been familiar. Adam's face hardened, his eyes showing anger. Or was it Kyle that woke me up? If Lucifer's blood is in my veins, his dark persona could've been familiar too. Adam looked back at the screen. "So why do you want us alive now?"

"I was wrong about your mental and emotional state," Matron said. "Seeing that you are not a threat, there is no need to kill you. There is a more pressing matter, of course, which I'm sure you're aware of."

Adam nodded. "Kyle."

"Yes, your ally, Kyle, is an obvious threat to Raquia. His power exceeds that of even the most exceptional human beings, and I believe he has received an amount far greater of the Demonic Harbinger's blood than even yourself. He is a threat to the rest of the world as well, and is therefore a problem that conflicts with both of my programmed interests. You are the only one capable of defeating him."

"He wants to awaken the Lucifer's... the Demonic Harbinger's power for himself," Adam said grimly.

"Opening the Demonic Harbinger's container in anyway will automatically activate the chamber's self-destruct system. How he would take the power for himself without opening the chamber is unknown."

Erin, Adam thought, she's got to be the key. Something about her has to be Kyle's way of getting that power. "Where is the Demonic Harbinger's chamber?"

The door Adam and Nathan had entered through reopened. "Follow the trail of dead," Matron said. "Kyle is already in the chamber."

"Nathan," Adam said, looking over his shoulder, "let's end this."

"I'm right behind you, Adam," Nathan said confidently.

The two men turned towards the door and walked towards it. Matron called after them just as Adam reached the door. "Adam. I am pleased to have met you. You are far different than who I thought you would be. Stop Kyle, and please, do not die."

Adam smiled faintly at the screen. "You probably should've said 'what you thought I would be,' but I appreciate your acknowledgement of me as a person." Adam and Nathan ran out of the room and down the blood stained hall, following the trail of dead bodies.

* * *

Kyle reached behind his back and pulled out his scythe, twirling it in his right hand as he faced the door, seeing movement far in the distance. His eyes glowed brilliantly, the yellow gleam visible far down the hallway. "Yes," he hissed. "Come to me." Kyle put his left hand into his pocket and grinned wickedly as Adam and Nathan came clearly into view.

Adam and Nathan entered the room, their faces hardened with determination and anger. Adam stretched his wings outward and Nathan turned off the safety on his pistol. "Kyle," the two men growled.

"Adam," Kyle said. "Nathan." He pulled his hand out of his pocket. "Welcome to the show."

Chapter XXIII

In Kyle's left hand was a small metal object the resembled the hilt of a sword. On the top was a blue button and coming from the bottom was a small rod that curved forward. "Do you know what this is, gentleman?" Kyle said, his brilliant yellow eyes darting back and forth between Adam and Nathan. "It was created to subdue Ahadiel if he ever got out of hand. It immobilizes those that have a significant trace of the Demonic Harbinger's blood." His thumb moved over the blue button. "Any in front of the rod become paralyzed."

Erin looked up wearily. Her vision was blurred, with the exception of one thing: Adam. He stood out perfectly, surrounded by a brilliant white aura that only she could perceive. "Adam," she said softly, "you came for me."

"Erin!" Adam shouted, his eyes widening. She's alive, he thought. He started to run forward but his body, as well as Nathan's, immediately became rigid and he fell to his knees, arms locked at his sides. All he could do was look ahead at Kyle's grinning face.

"Adam," Kyle cackled, "I'm really quite flattered that you decided to follow me. After all, what good is a party if the guest of honor doesn't show?" He tossed the metal object aside, and it broke as it hit the ground, the rod shattering and sparks flying from the bottom. He pulled out his pistol and pressed it against Erin's chest. "Now, let the festivities begin!"

"Adam," Erin whispered as a single tear rolled down her already soaked face. "I love you."

The single bullet rushed out of the barrel and tore through Erin, her heart exploding within her chest. The gunshot echoed throughout the room for what seemed to be an eternity as Erin's head slumped back down.

Adam's body remained frozen, but his eyes revealed what his body could not. Every bullet that had punctured his body, every blow that Ahadiel had delivered, the fire and acid that had burned his flesh and the agony of his father's voice in his head combined could not match the pain in his eyes. Adam saw the same visage he saw when Layla died. A brilliant red strand of hair formed in Adam's mind, surrounded by a warm light, filled with flashing images of Erin. Then, the strand snapped, and the light went away as blood soaked the broken hair.

Within the glass jar that Erin had been chained too, Lucifer's eyes glowed a faint yellow. Kyle held out his arms, ready to embrace the power of the demon. "Make me like God," he hissed. "Let this world burn!" Kyle looked over his shoulder at Adam. "And let this doll be the first to be consumed!"

The glow of Lucifer's eyes multiplied one hundred fold, filling the room. Kyle's body was engulfed in a brilliant flame and he fell to his knees screaming in an inhuman tone. Giant bat wings sprouted from his back, matching those of Lucifer's. Horns grew in identical locations on his face and his teeth became like knives. Finally, the glow faded, and the body within the jar was nothing more than a decaying corpse. Kyle rose to his feet, his laughter echoing throughout the room.

No, Adam thought.

No, I won't let this happen.

I won't let you do this.

God, are you there? Please, help me!

Adam's eyes watered as pain overwhelmed his body, his head feeling like it were about to explode.

I AM ALWAYS HERE, MY CHILD.

Father? You... recognize me?

The pain came back, but not even half as intense. As his father's voice boomed in his head, Adam's wings began to tingle.

YOU HAVE REMEMBERED YOURSELF, RAPHAEL. I HAD FEARED THAT I HAD LOST ANOTHER OF MY CHILDREN.

For a while, you had. I had died, but I was reborn, Father. I'm not Raphael anymore.

The pain was little more than a pinprick in Adam's skull now. His wings felt warm and tingled as if they had been asleep.

A NAME IS JUST A NAME. WHAT MATTERS IS HOW YOU PERCEIVE YOURSELF.

I perceive myself as Adam. As an angel who has fallen and risen up again. As a reminder that hope isn't lost to this world. As a friend.

The pain was gone, as was the tingling sensation, and Adam suddenly felt pure in a way that he had never felt before.

I CLEANSE YOU OF THE TAINTED BLOOD OF LUCIFER. NOW, FULFILL THE CHARGE YOU WERE GIVEN AGES AGO. PROTECT THIS WORLD FROM THE TAINT OF LUCIFER.

I won't fail, Father.

Now, Adam, you are truly reborn. There's no more need for me.

Raphael...

Go. Stop Kyle. I'll always be in your mind, living on as your memory.

And then the voice faded from Adam's mind, gone like a wisp of white smoke. Adam's eyes focused on Kyle, and he knew what had to be done.

"Kyle!" Adam screamed as his hands balled into fist and his wings spreading out to their fullest. Adam's blood boiled as his muscles strained to break from whatever spell they were under. Adam glared at Kyle who had spun around, astonished not only that Adam was able to move, but the appearance of his wings. Adam's wings were pure white and glowed brilliantly. Adam screamed and leapt off the ground, propelled by his wings, and fell towards Kyle.

"That's it, doll," Kyle hissed, his voice sounding more like an echo. "Come meet your death!" Kyle took his scythe in both hands and swung hard at Adam. The scythe crashed against Adam's right wing and sparks flew as it grinded across the length of the wing. Stepping to the side, Kyle brought his scythe over his head and swung it down at Adam's head. Adam braced himself and brought up his left wing as a shield. The scythe struck the top of the wing, but Kyle did not attempt another swing. His muscles rippled beneath his leather armor and he pressed forward, grinding his scythe against the wing. Adam felt his body begin to slip backwards and he slammed his left foot down hard and shoved back against Kyle.

"I won't let Lucifer be reborn," Adam hissed, his eyes blazing with pain and anger. "I won't let Erin be the tool for your petty ambition!" His right wing stretched out and locked in place when it straightened. "I won't let you hurt another person again!" Adam ducked down and spun his body so his right wing swung at Kyle's head.

Kyle stepped back and quickly moved his scythe to block Adam's wing. Sparks flew when the two collided, but neither man moved from the impact. "You won't take this from me too, doll!" His eyes mirrored Adam's pain and anger. "You took Layla from me! You won't take my revenge, too!" Kyle ducked down, moving his scythe to let Adam's wing swing past. Kyle stepped forward, raising his scythe high into the air, and swung at Adam's exposed back.

Adam spun in a circle, standing back up just in time to block the menacing scythe with his left wing. Adam stood sideways to Kyle, his head facing him. Kyle's face went red, a vein in his forehead pulsing wildly as he continued to grind his scythe against Adam, sparks shooting out sporadically. "I didn't kill Layla!" Adam snapped. "It was people like you that killed her!" Adam clenched his fists tight, his nails digging into his palms, blood pouring out. "People like you are the reason this world continues to rot!"

"Don't lecture me, doll!" Kyle screamed, glaring hard into Adam's eyes. "Layla was everything to me!"

"Erin was everything to me!" Adam screamed back even louder. "And you killed her!"

Adam and Kyle broke away from each other and began flying around the room. Kyle flapped his wings furiously, hurdling towards Adam. "Don't talk like you understand anything," Kyle screamed. "You're nothing but a worthless doll!"

Adam rolled his body to the side, the scythe missing by a fraction of an inch. Kyle slammed the pole end of the scythe into Adam's stomach, sending him spiraling to the ground. Adam managed to land on his feet just barely, using his wings to balance and shield him until he stood upright. "I'm not the one who's been manipulated," Adam shouted. "If anyone's a doll, it's you!"

Kyle landed in front of Adam and furiously swung his scythe again and again. Adam and Kyle never broke their gaze, yet Adam parried every one of Kyle's attacks. Kyle's scythe moved so fast it looked ethereal. Adam's wings matched the scythe's speed, appearing like a transparent white shield in front of Adam. Finally, as Kyle raised his scythe back for another stroke, Adam's wing followed it back. Adam's body moved forward and his right fist pounded against Kyle's stomach, followed by a left hook to Kyle's kidney. Adam grabbed Kyle's wrists and twisted them sharply and the scythe fell harmlessly onto the ground.

"Damn you!" Kyle screamed in pain, falling to his knees, his hands resting on the ground helplessly. "I hate you! I hate you!"

Adam grabbed Kyle's collar and lifted him off the ground, their eyes meeting for the last time. "Join your mighty Lucifer in Hell!" Adam threw Kyle at the glass jar that entombed Lucifer and his body crashed through the glass above Erin's corpse. The lighting in the room turned red and alarms filled the air.

"Warning!" a computerized voice echoed. "Demonic Harbinger's seal has been broken! Chamber self-destruct sequence initiated! Containing area in five. Four..."

Adam sprinted for the door, hearing Kyle screaming behind him. Adam grabbed the still rigid Nathan and pulled him along towards the closing door. As he ran, Adam saw tears in Nathan's eyes. Despite his paralysis, he had been forced to watch everything. Adam leapt through the door, holding Nathan tight, just in time for it to snap shut a bare inch behind him.

"Self-destruct sequence complete," the computerized voice echoed.

The hallway shook violently as a horrible explosion erupted within the chamber, so great that the door between Adam and Nathan and the chamber shattered, sending the two men flying forward as fire and shrapnel shot out through the door.

Slowly, Adam lifted himself off the ground and stood up, clutching his side. Nathan slowly began to regain his motor functions and leaned on his right elbow, his back off the ground as he looked back at the explosion.

"Erin," Nathan whispered, his eyes watering. "We couldn't save you."

Adam's eyes welled his tears and he fell back to his knees. The two men, surrounded by nothing more than corpses and debris, let go of all the tears they had ever held back.

Chapter XXIV

Adam and Nathan silently emerged from the long hallway and were greeted by a strangely warm sunlight, one that neither had ever experienced in the world below. The helicopter awaited them, sitting untouched on the landing strip. When the two men reached the helicopter, they stopped and looked at each other.

"So," Nathan said softly, "that's it." He looked down at the ground, his hand rubbing his forehead. "No happy ending, no joyous reunion. Just more pain, more loss." Nathan leaned back against the helicopter and sighed, his thumb and index finger clamping the corners of his eyes. "Kyle. Layla. Erin. Gone." He took a deep breath and sighed painfully. Adam didn't need to touch him to feel his sorrow. "We grew up together, us four, raised by Erin's mother. We were like family." Nathan pushed off from the helicopter and started walking towards the edge of the landing strip, followed shortly by Adam. He looked down at the white sea of clouds and then up at the sun. "Adam?" he said, holding back tears. "Do you think Erin is in heaven?"

Adam turned his head to look at Nathan. "I thought you didn't believe in that sort of thing."

Nathan looked back towards the clouds below. "I've lived my life by logic. Ever since I met you, I've seen so many things that defy logic." He turned his head and looked at Nathan. "But maybe those things didn't defy logic. Maybe they are logical. Maybe there is something more to all of this, something that I just can't see, and maybe it's illogical to believe that there isn't something out there watching." He looked back towards the sun, a single tear rolling down his right cheek. "Do you think Erin is in heaven?"

Adam smiled faintly, looking at his friend. He rested his hand on Nathan's shoulder and felt Nathan's sorrow slowly fade. "You know the answer to that."

Nathan still stared up at the sun. "Do you think this world will ever recover? Do you think the people will ever find hope again?"

Adam looked up at the sun, unmarred by dark clouds or never ending snow. He thought of Mecca and the great tribe it had housed. He thought of Erin and imagined how wonderful her mother must have been. Smiling faintly, he turned to Nathan. "The spirit can't be buried forever. It can be beaten, it can be stained, but it can't be destroyed. Catastrophe can quiet it, but nothing, not even death, can silence it." He turned towards the edge and made a sweeping gesture with his arm. "All of this... this pain, this suffering, this chaos... it's just a morning frost. Soon, the sun will shine, and everything will be beautiful again."